Beating it
WITH
BLOODY MARY

URBAN LEGEND EROTICA COLLECTION

Beating it
WITH
BLOODY MARY

HONEY CUMMINGS

4 Horsemen
Publications, Inc.

4 Horsemen Publications, Inc.
1497 Main St. Suite 169
Dunedin, FL 34698
4horsemenpublications.com
info@4horsemenpublications.com

Cover by Valerie Willis
Typesetting by Niki Tantillo
Edited by Heather Teele

Library of Congress Control Number: 2023931135

Paperback ISBN-13: 978-1-64450-170-2
Audiobook ISBN-13: 978-1-64450-837-4
Ebook ISBN-13: 978-1-64450-159-7

Dedication

To an amazing team for always beating it! You know, deadlines, corrections, and all those naughty tribulations!

Table of Contents

1

A Storm Was Coming

MARY

Mary couldn't remember how she ended up imprisoned inside this dark place or anything else about herself—not even her last name. *This blows.* Everywhere in the pitch-black abyss looked like stars sparkling, fading in and out without a pattern. Upon further inspection, Mary discovered candles and flashlights coming from behind pools of dark mirrors which held strange faces and unknown places. Each portal was a copy of the mirror on her side, whether a medicine cabinet, hand mirror, or even large wooden heirloom mirrors.

They come in waves; it's always dark as night on their side, and they are terrified out of their minds. No matter who they were or where they came from, they whispered the same thing from all directions as she stood in an endless space where she was neither dead nor living. *I suppose I was terrified when I used to dabble in the occult too.*

"Bloody Mary, Bloody Mary, Bloody Mary."

1

Did I die and become Bloody Mary? Am I in some sort of Purgatory or... Her chest ached as she dropped to her knees. *Is this my personal Hell? Did I do something terrible? Why can't I remember?*

"Hell Mary, Hell Mary, Hell Mary."

Her heart throbbed inside her chest as she searched the mirrors of murmurs, all saying her name in one manner or another, some less dark than others. *I've been here for so long that I've lost track of time. Should I just give up entirely on the idea of escaping?*

"Mary Worth, Mary Worth, Mary Worth. Nothing is happening. Ugh."

Sometimes, they whispered it three times; other times, they performed the chant ten times. *Five. I think the number is five when it does something different.* Others squinted their eyes at the mirror, looking through her as she pushed on the glass and beat her fists against it in hopes something would change. Smells, warmth, and even a ripple in the mirror would hint something was happening on that fifth repeat of her name.

Please, tell me some of them can see me trapped in this dark tower of mirrors? At times, she would lock eyes, and for a fleeting moment, a look of recognition and fear would cross their faces before they ran away or the mirror dissolved like dust in the wind. In those moments, she tried to escape but found she couldn't even get a strand of hair to cross the glass of the mirror.

Flopping onto her back, Mary huffed. *I'm so overdressed for this bullshit.* She fought with the red skirts of what looked more like a prom dress than a dress for a gala or cocktail party. Her halter top fit snugly enough not to slip easily down her torso, but it left little protection from the chill that crept through this wall-less prison. *I'm so bored.* She glanced over at a mirror; the bluish glow emanating from it made her arch a brow. A flick of a finger brought the mirror closer. *At least I mastered that trick. Before, I was walking a mile to get to one.*

A broad-shouldered man was beating on a door while holding a glowing rectangle. "Hey! Don't do this," he roared. "You can't lock me in here all night!"

Propping up on her elbows, she snorted to herself. *Is that a smartphone? I suppose that counts as a flashlight.* She bit her lip in thought. *He hasn't said my name, so why can I hear and see him?*

"Come on! I know hazing is outdated, but this is still hazing guys!" He flopped his back against the door and slid to the floor. "At least I have my cell phone," he mumbled.

"Cell phone?" Mary lurched forward to sit fully. "Since when did they stop looking like glowing, building bricks? How long have I fucking been here for him to say it's a mere cellphone? I mean, when I was there, it was cell phone and the smart phone. And what was it? Ah, yes, the iPhone and Omnia?" She called the mirror even closer, squinting her eyes into the darkness in hopes of getting a better look. "Man, why do I have to watch technology improve with no means to play with it?"

A loud huff escaped the man as he glared down at his phone, occasionally tapping his thumb on it. He looked Latino with hazel eyes, a five o'clock shadow, and a bald-fade haircut. A strong jawline led her eyes to his pronounced Adam's apple and collarbone that peaked out of his wide-neck, raglan shirt. The sleeves were pushed up to his elbows, exposing strong forearms and angular wrist bones. The clean-cut college boy dripped of masculinity.

"Hello, sir." Mary held the edges of the old, vintage, body mirror, her body warming with arousal at the eye candy before her. "But he hasn't said my name or the chant? Well, who am I not to take advantage of this moment and enjoy myself for once." She bit her lip, contemplating the mischievous deeds and desires stirring at her core. "I've been inadvertently summoned countless times by women named Mary being fucked within sight of a mirror. I mean, it's not like he can see me." Hissing, she continued to think out loud. "Does this make me some kind of creepy pervert? I just need some visuals to get off..."

Knocking on the closet door made them both jolt. "We need to hear you say it, CJ!" someone shouted.

"Fine." Exasperated, CJ mumbled something quickly under his breath.

"LOUDER!" The cackling from the unseen group annoyed Mary as much as it did CJ. "And you better be in front of the mirror."

"You better let me out of this closet after this," growled CJ as he looked around the room.

She could have sworn their eyes met, and it made her face flush. He shuffled closer, and she held her breath as if he might discover her and her naughty thoughts. Reaching out, he gripped the mirror in the same place she held it. A warm sensation hit her hands, and she let go, gasping. *What the hell was that? Is he some sort of wizard?* Glaring at the mirror, his eyes had lost hers, and a pang of regret ached in her chest. In fact, she swore she could feel the heat of his body through the magic of the mirror, and her body throbbed with want.

I must be beyond horny to be so sensitive to his every look and touch. To feel the heat of a man in my arms again... Licking her lips, she pulled her skirt up, hands trailing up her inner thighs as she began to play with herself. *I'm doing it. Even if he sees me for a moment, it's not like he knows I'm a real person desperate to cum.* Her pussy slick with anticipation, she circled her pink pearl. *Oh, I'm more than ready...* A jolt of pleasure shot through her, and his eyes locked on hers. *It's been so long.* She held her breath. *Don't look away... I'm so into this moment... Please don't look away.* Her fingers slid back down, dipping inside, and she inhaled swiftly with a wave of pleasure.

"Bloody Mary." His voice was deep, and his eyes were on her as he spoke her name. "Bloody Mary."

Mary inhaled deeply as she retreated to her clit, circling ever faster. "That's it, baby." He licked his lips, clearing his throat. "Keep saying my name." She exhaled as she began to edge on the verge of an orgasm. "Oh, how I wish we could hook up right here and now."

"Bloody Mary," he called to her, his voice low and provocative. "Bloody Mary."

Her fingers dipped inside her flower, and she hummed. *So close... don't stop... one more time...* she pleaded in silence, eyelids heavy as she retreated once more, circling as she inhaled. Each movement was more sensitive than the last. The electric shock of pleasure made her flinch and shake. The scent of cologne filled the air, sending a shiver through her body. *It's almost as if he can touch me. Please touch me...* She closed her eyes as the peak of her orgasm teasingly teetered just out of reach. *So close...*

"Bloody Mary." The deep roll of his voice made her inhale.

"Fuck, yes!" she exclaimed as she climaxed, dipping her fingers deep into her pussy, stroking fast and hard.

His hands passed through the mirror's threshold, and he fell toward her. "What the fuck!" he shouted.

The weight and feel of him on top of her added to her climax, and she crested higher. "Fuck me!" she squealed in ecstasy.

Her thighs attempted to close but found a man's hot torso between them. Wide-eyed, she glared up at him, and in her lust, gripped his shirt and pulled him closer. He didn't refuse; as their lips met, she deepened the kiss. As if caught in her spell, she could hear him unbuckling and unzipping. The heat of his hand rubbing her swollen pussy made her grind against his fingers, and he moaned in her lips, tongues entangled. He pulled away, biting her lip before freeing his hard cock from his pants. Both panted with erotic excitement.

"Who are you?" He had come to his senses and tried to retreat, but her ankles locked behind him.

"Does it matter?" With her heart pounding, her mind raced with how to keep him there. *I can't let this chance pass me.* "Fuck me. I want you so badly. Please, fuck me."

"I don't know who you are..." She tugged him closer, wrapping her thighs tightly around his hard planes. "But you're not gonna let me leave." A haphazard smirk crossed his face, and at last, naughty desires flashed in his eyes. "I'm CJ; I assume you're Mary?" he offered.

"Fuck me, CJ," she demanded, earning a growl in response as he contemplated the offer.

"Please tell me your name is Mary." CJ's eyes snaked down her body before resting on the apex of her thighs where his hands slid, slow and hot to her throbbing desire. "So wet..."

"You summoned me; now give me what I want," she commanded.

"I thought you took souls," he snorted. His fingers slid over her opening before dipping his long, thick fingers inside her channel.

Her face flushed, and she snarked, "Well, the Victorians thought this was soul-taking, so let's die a little tonight."

"You have no idea how lucrative that sounds to an English major with a Victorian Era history understudy." CJ sucked on a cheek with a look of wonder on his face. "Who are you?"

"Don't tell anyone, but I'm really into nerds." Turning her head away, her commanding attitude began to falter. *Shit, I can't.* Squeezing her eyes shut, she cursed herself. *Fuck, fuck, fuck! He's going to leave before I even get his cock inside me!*

2

Beyond the Limit of Their Bond

CJ

The girl was pale, almost glowing in the darkness of the closet. CJ Galdur struggled to make out his surroundings, but he couldn't tear his eyes away from the lustful beauty he found himself on top of. *Am I still in the closet? Is this the plan: get the new fraternity brother laid? I'm game for that. She's fucking gorgeous and ready to go!* Black tendrils of hair fanned out framing her flushed cheeks and deep red lips. Her dark eyes and alluring voice cut through him. She had gotten him hard instantly. *How did I not notice her in the closet with me? What kind of girl is willing to bang the new guy and be ready...*

He grabbed her chin, turning her eyes back to his. "I want your eyes on me, Mary."

He pressed the top of his cock against her opening and her breath caught, thighs squeezing him in anticipation. Slowly, he rocked his hips forward, and he watched her arch along with him. The strapless red dress in the dark closet made her look like a long-forgotten deity of desire. Her pussy tightened around his hard shaft as he pushed deeper inside her wet heat until he was buried to his hilt. A moan escaped her as she rocked against him, pulsing and throbbing, edging him closer to an orgasm.

Leaning down and kissing her neck, he whispered, "I wasn't expecting to take the flyers [1] today..."

She retorted, "And I wasn't expecting the town bull to wreck my china shop today."

They paused and chuckled over it before he shook his head, meeting her gaze. "Who are you?"

"Doesn't matter." Mary squeezed her channel tight around his cock, swaying her hips and making him shudder. "Now, give me a bit of your soul, would you kindly?"

Locking lips, she suckled on his tongue as he began fucking her, slow and steady. Pulling back just far enough for the ridge of his cap to catch the muscles at her opening, CJ teased her by hovering there. At last, agonizingly slowly, he slid deep into her, hips connecting once more. He slid in and out, slowly still. Mary wiggled with frustration.

"Faster, harder," she pleaded.

"Patience," he admonished.

Weaving his arms under her, he managed to find the top latch and zipper at the back of her dress. The heat of her hands slid under his shirt, gliding over the ripples of his ribs before clawing at his back. Ramming hard and fast inside her, he tugged the dress down to expose her breasts and mocha-colored areolas. Mary arched, nails scratching across his shoulder blades in reply.

---

[1] Figure of speech meaning to take a chance against the odds, or make a choice without knowing the outcome

She moaned as her legs shook. Her honey dripped between them with each motion, spurring him on to keep her exploding.

Biting Mary's lip, CJ sucked it playfully as if teasing her about where he aimed to be next. She wiggled on his hard cock as he kissed down her porcelain neck, white as snow, leaving red and purple blossoms leading downward until he reached her nipple. Lips wrapped around the bud as the tip of his tongue circled. CJ snaked a hand between her legs, finding her clit with his thumb. She bucked in reply, and he let go of her swollen nipple.

"Keep that up and we might really blow off the groundsills," he mocked with another circle and buck.

"Shit, I shouldn't have tossed off before..." Her breath caught as his cock jumped inside her.

His smile widened. "You started without me? How long have they had you in this closet?"

"I don't want to talk about it." Her thighs squeezed as she tightened around his throbbing member inside her. "Fuck me until we die, you nerd."

"As you wish, Bloody Mary," he cooed, leaning down to suckle on the other nipple.

Circling his thumb on her clit, he could feel her drawing ever closer to another orgasm. She kept trying to say something but couldn't; she tightened and jolted as he played with her more aggressively. Catching her nipple in his teeth, he tugged and pinched. A gush and pulsing teamed with her cry. He had set her orgasm into full bloom, reaching a new height. Riding his hands up her legs, he found her hips hidden deep in the red curtains of the dress and began hammering her, hard and fast. She arched until she lifted off the ground, lifting her knees for deeper penetration. As her nails dug deep into his back, he pulled out, stroking as he came across her red dress and breasts.

CJ moaned. His eyes stayed on her as he came, cum sparkling across her body underneath him. "Sorry, not ready for basket making." He gave a coy smile as he continued the exchange of dated terms.

She threw her hand over her face, chuckling. "And this is my only dress... so that's going to be interesting."

CJ leaned back and knelt between her open legs. "If that's the case, I owe you a dress. That was ... amazing."

She frowned. She opened her mouth to say something but clamped shut fast. Frustrated by the sudden sour shift, he began rubbing between her swollen, hot petals. She gasped and gripped his wrist in alarm. His fingertips played with her hardened pearl and teased the weeping gash.

"Don't... I don't think, oh!" she gasped, stopping her words.

Her strength didn't stop him from dipping two fingers inside, stroking. A visceral scream escaped her, and her knees clamped hard into his ribs as she came again. Her orgasm, violent and sudden, exploded with a gush of fluid as she came. Not satisfied, CJ didn't stop until her voice hit a new pitch and a fountain exploded forth. Her fingers tight on his wrist, she stared up, wide-eyed and panting.

"What did you do to me?" She marveled over what he had summoned forth. "Th-that's a first. So many firsts, but that..."

"If you misbehave and get sad, I'll have to do it again to teach you a lesson," he warned, hazel eyes glowing in the abyss as he licked his fingers. "You understand?"

"Oh, you're something else." She looked at her dress, now wet and cum-stained, and smirked. "Something to remember you by?"

"Maybe, but..." Tucking himself away, he spun around and began searching the floor. "I want your number to take you out on a proper date." He found his phone by the door and unlocked it to see several missed calls and messages. "Damn, didn't even notice everyone blowing it up." Spinning around, he found himself alone. "M-Mary?"

He was met with silence as he stared at his reflection in the mirror; cum was splattered across the glass. *What the fuck?* Crawling back, he looked behind it and felt all around the closet in a panic. *Where the hell did she go? Don't tell me there's a door over here. Nothing.* His heart thudded hard in his chest, and he read the texts he had missed.

[FratBoss: Where the fuck r u?] Friday, October 13, 11:33 a.m.

[Mark: How da fuck u get out of a locked closet?] Saturday, October 14, 1:12 a.m.

[FratBoss: Not cool man. Where did u go?] Saturday, October 14, 2:45 a.m.

[Timmah: Dude. Call me when you get back. We need to talk.] Saturday, October 14, 3:33 a.m.

[Unknown: Hey this is Geo. Frat Boss is looking for you. Call him at 321-555-1234 in case you don't got his number bro] Saturday, October 14, 2:41 p.m.

[Mark: I'm in a situation. Heard you ghosted the fraternity after haze. We'll talk when I get back to normal. I'm with Tim trying to figure out what the fuck he did to me.] Sunday, October 15, 7:23 p.m.

[Timmah: Look, don't do anything too crazy until I get back. I fucked up man, the hazing for you and Mark, it backfired. Please tell me you're alive.] Sunday, October 15, 8:37 p.m.

[School: You were reported absent today.] Monday, October 16, 7:48 a.m.

[FratBoss: It's been 2 days. Plz call me ASAP.] Monday, October 16, 9:45 a.m.

He swallowed; time didn't make sense anymore. "Was I in this closet whacking off to the mirror for three days? What the fuck did they slip in my fucking drink?"

[CJ: What the fuck did you put in my drink]

[FratBoss: Where r u?]

CJ stood and tried to open the closet, but it remained lock. [CJ: Still in the closet, asshole]

He heard a huge scuffle, and the door swung open. Everyone was dumbfounded as they looked at one another. *What the hell is going on?* Relief filled their faces, and they all started to laugh; the fraternity leader and a professional student of almost twenty years, Jason, patted him on his shoulder. CJ furrowed his brow, looking back to the closet and to his phone. *It's almost completely dead at three percent, yet I had a full charge when I went in here.* His stomach knotted.

"Man, that's a damn good prank," reassured Jason. "You didn't mention you were a magician; that's impressive."

CJ looked over them, not sure what to say. "No one slipped something in my drink, did they? Acid? Peyote? Shrooms?"

There was another exchange of visibly confused faces.

"No, man," Geo spoke up, throwing his hands up. "They would shut the whole fraternity down and kick us out of school over that."

CJ scrolled through his phone and asked, "Where's Timmy? Wasn't he the one that set this up?"

"You know," hummed Jason, looking overly thoughtful. "When did that short bastard haul ass on us?"

"He said something about Mark," answered CJ. "The last guy that just joined the frat, right?"

"Oh, shit, Marky-Mark?" Geo waved a hand. "He swapped the Lady in Blue Ghost Challenge days and figured it would cheer the poor guy up. His girl got caught fucking an Abraxus Tasker College kicker, so he set him up for a wild weekend."

Maybe that's it. They just hook us up with one-night stands, thought CJ.

"Wasn't that this weekend?" Jason arched a brow.

CJ pushed through them, tapping on his cell phone and ignoring anything else they had to offer. *If Timmy set this up, he must know her. I could not care less for these asshats.*

[CJ: I need Mary's number. Now.]

[Timmah: Who the hell is Mary? I don't currently know anyone named Mary. Did she mention me?]

Covering his mouth, CJ glared at himself in the hallway mirror. *Was it a dream?* Lifting his shirt, he could see the scratches, and a shudder rolled over him. *Who the hell is Mary? And how do I find her?*

3

If Love is Perfect

MARY

Tugging up her dress, Mary muttered curses under her breath. "My legs are like a newborn deer, and I'm a wreck." Smirking, she raised her eyebrows high and confessed, "At least I got laid. That hasn't happened since..." her voice trailed off. *All I know is, I've been here.*

Wiggling her body, she shimmied the dress until it slid up, covering her breasts. Looking down, she scoffed. *I'm still ... sticky. Great. I should have locked my ankles harder so he would have cum some place less ... messy. It's not like a ghost woman can get knocked up. I mean, if I am Bloody Mary, right? But I don't have any other dress or clothes. Fuck my life.*

Reaching behind her, Mary groaned. Her arms stretched behind, doing battle with the open flaps of her gown. She couldn't get the zipper all the way up, let alone latch it. *Are you kidding me? Am I going to face the next few decades holding this dress up? Had to pick a halter top, didn't you, Mary? Straps aren't sexy, and this has easy off and on features. My ass!* Frustrated, she tucked the skirt between her legs to sop up the wetness that had dribbled down them. *Maybe I can get him back here to help me out...*

"Who was that magical man?" Looking at the twinkling mirrors that spanned across the darkness, she noticed one brighter than the rest. "Is... is that daylight?" She flicked a finger, and it shot across the room and paused to float before her. "You got to be fucking kidding me?"

The reflection was indeed daylight, and much to her delight, CJ stood on the other side of the pool. He lifted his shirt, exposing the marks she had left behind in her ecstasy. A smile crested her face, and he smiled in unison. *I guess we both left a little something to remember each other by. Shame he didn't take me with him.* Her heart broke as he walked out of view. *Maybe one day, we can...* The pain made her drop back to the floor, clutching her disheveled skirt.

Looking down at her dress Mary cringed. *Ah, how am I going to shower here? I'm just a cum-covered apparition in the mirror now. Gross.* She frowned before making herself laugh. *How ridiculous is this whole situation?* Her anxiety tightened in her chest and throat again, and she shook her head. *Think about something else,* she demanded to herself.

"Time passes fast over there, doesn't it? I've seen faces age in a matter of weeks. Is it that time has no meaning anymore and weeks were really years? I have no idea if it's been a few hours or days since we..." Her heart leapt to her throat, and she fought to hold back the tears. "How easily will you forget me, mystery man who entered this place and left as soon as you wished? Hmmm, CJ?"

With a wave of her hand, she called forth an assortment of mirrors. *If I can only track him. He's at least interesting enough, no? Will he call my name again? Even then, will I hear it among a thousand others?* Giving chase to him proved difficult.

Ignoring the echoes and mutters of those trying to summon her, she searched for him and his voice among the waves of glittering pools. Candles came and went like fluttering fireflies. Flashlights beamed like lighthouses which had lost their purpose and no longer functioned to salvage the lost souls at sea or warn of rocky shores.

"This is pointless," she murmured in defeat.

Waving her arm, the mirrors soared away, and Mary began her aimless march. *Where the hell are my shoes?* The dress started sliding down, and she yanked it up. *Ugh, this marble floor is cold, and that old carpet that appears on occasion is gross. Blegh.* Turning at random, the mirrors grew in size as she clenched her teeth. *There must be more portals to look through, more to this place than I realize. If he can travel here and leave, maybe I just need to find the mirror I came through.* Another tug of the dress and she stumbled to a stop, spinning to look at all the mirrors behind her. A flash of the Terracotta Army came to mind, and she scoffed.

"How did I get here?" she shouted, but her voice didn't even echo in the emptiness. "I WANT THE FUCK OUT," she screeched, straining her voice to the point of breaking.

Closing her eyes, she searched her memories. A song played from a nearby mirror, though a new decade had passed since she last heard it. *That's right, I've heard this song. I loved this song.* Adjusting the skirts, she sat down with her elbows on her thighs and propped her face on her hands. Holding onto the nostalgic sensation working itself into knots at her core, she pushed to uncover the fuzzy flashbacks lingering just out of reach. *That's right, that night, at the dance...*

"Mary, I thought you were coming with Jason?" A voice from her past shook her awake.

Opening her eyes, she found herself in front of a mirror, lipstick in hand. "W-wait..." Blinking, she stared at her reflection and dropped the bright red stick. "I'm..."

Startled, she watched as lipstick smudged the snow-white sink and turned to find herself in a public restroom. *I've seen this place before.* Outside the doors, she could hear the familiar song, yet behind her, the entire wall was covered by a massive mirror. A shudder raced over her body. Her heart leapt, and she backed up against the bathroom stalls. Someone shrieked in the stall behind her.

"Damnit, Mary! That scared me!" A toilet flushed, and a blonde-haired girl with green eyes frowned as she stepped out from the stall. "So, Jason... he finally ditch you?"

"I..." Shuffling out of her way, she arrived at the sink and frowned at the lipstick. "Sorry, I'm not ... myself?" Mary locked eyes with her reflection, and it flashed as if seeing herself in the abyss. "I don't know what the fuck is happening right now."

"Look, sorry I didn't say anything about it, but you know how the debutants are around here." The girl scoffed, washing her hands. "Man, why'd you drop the lipstick? I wanted to put that shade on."

Mary shook her head, bolting out of the bathroom into the crowd of party goers. Clutching her chest, she spun in the crowd, lost in the roar of music and her beating heart. A disco ball spun overhead; lights of all colors scattered over the crowd, everyone dressed like they were attending a high school prom. Every girl wore a fluffy skirt or heavy dress—popular in the late 80s or early 90s. Pushing through people, Mary made it to a buffet table. An assortment of alcohol took up most of the real estate, and she leaned on it.

Was it a dream? Or did someone slip something to me? Slapping her cheeks, she stared at the banner on the table: "Party like it's 1999."

"Is that you, Mary?" A male voice made her heart flutter. She turned, hoping for CJ but found a stranger. "Where's Jason? I thought you two..."

"N-not here," she stuttered. Mary tucked a lock of hair behind her ear, and her eyes darted down to her now clean dress. "I'm sorry; I must be going."

"Uh oh." He gripped her arm before she could leave. "Did he finally break up with you?"

Shit, I can't remember ... anything. Tears welled up in her eyes from frustration. "I need to sit down; I'm not feeling so great."

"Look, I mean, we all knew." He let go, and she darted back through the crowd.

Why don't I remember these people? What year is it? Where am I? Shoving out double doors, she found herself alone in a hallway. *There are no lockers, so this isn't a high school.* Walking down the hall, she searched the posters and flyers for clues. *There!* She doubled back to a flyer. *2013. These have events for 2013 and college dorm news and more. I'm a college student. But is this the present or past? Does CJ even exist?*

"Mary." The voice startled her, and she twisted to face him. "I thought you left?" He was handsome, and her heart fluttered at the man before her—blue eyes, blonde hair, and tanned skin, all packaged in a tuxedo. "Nevermind that," he deflected, glancing down and away. "Look, if I knew you were coming, we, well, I would have..."

"Jason." His name fell from her lips as a wall of bitter emotions exploded in her core. "I don't care anymore."

"Excuse me?" He met her gaze, knitting his brow in confusion. "Mary, I know you're confused about why I broke it off with you yesterday, but—"

Her chest stung, and she cut him off. "But nothing! I've already forgotten you, and it's not like you've come looking for me." Mary clamped her lips closed. *He doesn't know I've been trapped. This is just a memory in a mirror. He probably just thinks I left to save face or dropped out and ghosted everyone.*

"I see." Jason's tone softened, and he turned his back to her. "Sorry, I saw you rush out here and thought it was because you saw me. I was mistaken. Look, I'll see you at the after party at our frat house." And with that, he stomped off, shoving through the double doors back into the party.

I wasn't important enough for you to even remember when I went missing, she mouthed to herself as a tear slid down her cheek. *I want someone to at least remember me and sincerely miss me.*

The hallway lights started to flicker, and the room grew darker. Closing her eyes, Mary steeled herself for her return to the abyss of starlight-by-mirror. The music had allowed her to relive a moment, faded and long gone. The hurried whispers of those calling her name replaced it as the mirror dissipated, lost to the void once more. Goosebumps rolled over her as she began to walk aimlessly again. Her bare feet slapped against the black marble. Emotions were goading her to go someplace— anywhere new—as she paced meaninglessly. Again, she tugged her dress back up on her hips; the back had unzipped again, and though she tried once more, she was still unable to reach the top.

A smile crept across her face as her body buzzed with wanton desire. *You know, maybe CJ might miss me? At least for a fleeting moment, I wasn't alone anymore...*

4

If Hate is Perfect

CJ

Staring into the rearview mirror, CJ found himself waiting. *For who? What exactly...* Ripping his eyes away, he drummed his fingers on the steering wheel. *Why can't I forget about Mary?*

It had been weeks since his sexual rendezvous with the mysterious lady in the mirror. Chills rolled over him, and he shuddered them off. His mind wandered back to her soft skin, the rustling of her red dress, and the sound of her voice, still sharp. When he closed his eyes, he could still feel the heat of her lips and the warmth of her thighs pressing on him. She haunted his dreams, and he woke cold and covered in sweat. Even with the top down on his convertible Corvette and the hot sun bearing down on him, he couldn't stop shivering from a combination of excitement and fear. Nothing seemed to cut through the unease that knotted his gut about what he wouldn't allow himself to consider.

What and who she might actually be is... The flirty and lust-loving side of him had died that night when he crossed back from the world on the other side of the mirror. *Was it all an illusion? Did I have a mental break down? But the scratches, the kiss, the sex...* A heat washed over him, and he cleared his throat, shaking his head. *If I keep circling back like this, I'm going to be at full salute,* he jeered at himself and stared across the street.

"Hey, baby!" A petite, busty girl sashayed up to the car with her posse of debutants hot on her heels. "Sorry, it took me a little while to finish shopping with the girls." They giggled in unison as she flicked a strand of short, red hair from her eyes. "See you later, ladies." She swayed her hips until she was at the passenger door and reprimanded, "Babe, the door?"

"It's unlocked, Chelsea," he drawled.

"Babe..." she lowered her voice, sneering, "the girls are watching."

"They're always watching," he deadpanned as she looked back at her posse with a nervous laugh. "You're not even carrying anything, and you called me to come get you, so here I am."

Giving him a disapproving glare, Chelsea jerked open the car door and slammed it behind her. "You're embarrassing me."

Whispers and gossip erupted, but he put the car in drive and squealed down the street. Whatever he saw in her before was lost. It had been an empty relationship—always one sided with her side being the only one benefitting from their relationship. His thoughts drifted as she jabbered on about nothing of importance. CJ didn't say a word to Chelsea as she carried on the conversation about her newly-dyed red hair, the upcoming annual frat and sorority gala, what she expected him to do for her, and how embarrassing it was that he couldn't at least *open the damn car door* for her. Relief washed over him as they pulled in front of her driveway—a rental property he assumed Daddy's money paid for since she didn't have a card in her wallet that carried her own name.

"I'm sorry, are you mad at me?" Chelsea cooed, leaning over to kiss his cheek. "I didn't mean to get so mad at you, baby. How about you come inside…" she said, shifting to a sultry voice and whispering in his ear, "the house and me." The mood swing was knee-jerking to him as she continued pawing at him. "I'll make it up to you if you make it up to me." She bit teasingly now, nibbling and licking his ear.

"No, just got something on my mind." CJ stole another glance at the rearview mirror. *Nothing.* She bit harder as if demanding a reaction against his will. "Chelsea, stop." Her hand slid over his thigh and snaked toward his crotch. "I said stop." He pushed her off and glared at her. "I don't think—"

"What's your problem?" Chelsea snapped, crossing her arms. "What did they do to you during their hazing ritual? Did they not have a warden or chaplain? I mean, at least a marshal present? Maybe I should have a word with Jason."

"What the hell does Jason have to do with our relationship?" Shaking his head, CJ locked eyes with her. "Every time you seem unhappy with me or something I'm unwilling to do, you threaten to see him as if he's in charge of every decision I make. What does my fraternity president have to do with our relationship?"

"Look, I'm trying to be the best girlfriend, but if this keeps up CJ, we can't be together." She tsked and opened the car door. "I have a reputation to keep. At least your frat boss gets that; I don't know what I was thinking settling with you. Rumors are going to start getting around, and you know how I feel about gossip."

"You mean you want to be the one dealing out the gossip," he corrected. "Not on the receiving end. I don't give a shit what they think. This isn't fucking high school."

Chelsea rolled her eyes, and her scowl deepened. "I hate to tell you, but without me, you'd be nothing. Don't forget we have a gala; I expect you to spare no expense."

"Yeah, I got you. I'll be your little cheese boy one last time," he spat in reply. "But after that, I'm done putting on airs for the debutants who you worship so dearly. You can go get cash from your little fuck boy Jason from now on."

They glared at each other for a moment as her mouth opened and closed like a fish with no voice. At last, she marched off, almost falling when one of her heels caught the crack between the two concrete slabs of the sidewalk. CJ's temper burned as he peeled out into the road and headed home.

What relationship? he thought bitterly. *We both came from money, and it has been more of an arranged relationship, for what? Gossip? Sure, it's been fun fooling around, but now, it's more trouble than it's worth. Besides, I think I've fallen for Mary. Whoever she is, she must be an English major. History or anthropology minor, at the very least?* He pushed the garage button, and it started to open as he pulled up the driveway. *She caught all those references so maybe a minor in Victorian Era culture? Literature?*

Putting the Corvette in park, CJ leaned on the steering wheel in defeat. The garage went dark as the door closed; the hot, stale air reminded him of the closet all those weeks ago. *Dammit, just thinking about it...* He puffed out his cheeks as his pants tightened from the rise of his cock. *Fuck it.* He marched for his bathroom, tossing clothes off as he made his way through the house. Slamming the water knob, the shower sputtered to life. The cold splashes made him flinch but did nothing to quell the arousal and heat of lust building from his core.

Leaning into the water, eyes tight, he began stroking his hard dick. Flashes of her red dress and the way her pale body blossomed out from the folds of the skirt made him moan.

Licking his lips, his thumb rolled over the tip of his shaft as he thought about the kiss they had shared. The water grew warmer at last, and his balls tightened.

So close... Edging, at the cusp of an orgasm, a moan escaped him. He muttered naughty desires, stroking faster and firmer. *She was so wet...* He let his mind wander back to how her hot, tight pussy squeezed around his cock as he entered her. His dick throbbed as the tight, tingling sensation began to build. *That's it... just a little more.* He moaned again as he drew near the edge. A sharp ache cut through him before he could release, his body betraying him.

"Fuck me." He slammed the knob and shut the water off.

Frustration filled him as he marched angrily into his bedroom, water dripping off his chin and body. He froze. Slowly turning, he focused his attention on the mirrored wall. Arching a brow, another wave of provocation beckoned him and his cock, making him throb with desire once more. Licking his teeth, he stared up at the ceiling, hesitant to let himself act upon the lustful wants of his body and mind.

"What the hell do I have to lose?" CJ smirked, allowing himself to catch his own devilish expression. *I mean, I'm just beating it with Bloody Mary. It's not like anyone is watching me, and, even then, I wouldn't mind an audience.* A shudder of exhilaration fluttered over him. *Even sexier if she can see me...*

A chill of excitement crawled up his spine as he approached. Leaning an arm on the mirror, he let the tip of his cock touch and rub the cool glass of the mirror's surface. Closing his eyes, he tilted his hips, so the underside rode up the glass, and by the third tilt, it began to slide on precum. Edging closer, he feared rushing it. The mirror was warm from his efforts, almost vibrating as pleasure rolled through him. Muscles through his body tightened.

"Mary," he moaned, daring to reach down and begin stroking, pressing his cock firmer onto the mirror. "Bloody Mary."

Eyelids heavy, he stared past himself, deep into the depths of the abyss where a haze of red looked watery in the rise of his ecstasy. He could smell her perfume. Moaning as his arousal teetered on the edge again, he didn't want to peak just yet. *Just a little longer.* His reflection seemed to have dissipated as he rubbed the shaft up the glass before retreating. Rolling a thumb over the weeping tip of his cock, he glanced down to see the tip pressed against its mirrored doppelganger. *Let me linger on the edge, let me see her before...* Thoughts of her rolled forward. *The way her legs wrapped around me and how she rocked, making me catch my breath.* The pleasure of the head sliding against the glass left him wanting. *I just want to see...*

5

Stainless Bride of Stainless King

Mary

"Bloody Mary." His voice cut through the overwhelming storm of mirrors and people calling to her.

"CJ, I found you, but..." Mary paused a moment, fearing that time had lurched forward in this endless eternity where she couldn't grasp if she lived in the past, present, or future. "Please, let me have this much."

"Bloody Mary." Again, the provocative way he spoke her name sent goosebumps across her skin.

She waved the mirror to her. The room was dark behind him. Droplets of water beaded down his body in rivulets. He seemed of the same age, but she couldn't tell in the lack of light. His forehead leaned against the mirror, and he stood naked before her. Steam painted the glass, disappearing only to reappear with each labored breath. The muscles in his body were taut as he edged closer to an orgasm; the muscles in his forearm flexed as he stroked his cock, pressing it against the glass.

"Oh, say it one more time for me." Pressing against the glass, she could feel the heat of his body through it and wished either of them could push through the cold, hard threshold that kept them divided by nothing more than ill-fated magic. "Five times, my love. Once more and perhaps one of us can touch the other like that night."

"So close," he muttered, rubbing against the mirror with the tip of his cock, slick with precum as he moaned.

Mary's fingers slid between her thighs, rubbing the folds of her pussy. The tip of her finger found her clit before riding her pink crevasse to dive into the wet depths. Pulling back her honey across the pink jewel, she began to pleasure herself along-side him. *If I can't fuck him, I'll gladly play with myself as I watch him cum across my mirror.* His eyes shut as she waited, agonizing over wanting him to call her name for a fifth and final time. He bit his lip and repositioned in front of her—palms overhead and body flat against the mirror as he rubbed his cock against the glass, enjoying the sensation. She inhaled swiftly as CJ fucked the mirror with thoughts of her in his mind and on his lips.

"Open your eyes and call my name, please." Pleading, she drank him in before letting her own dress drop to the floor. "My Adonis, let us lose a little more of our souls together again." Mary knelt before him, the glass a cruel reminder she couldn't escape this prison.

A moan escaped him, and he murmured her name at last, "My Mary."

The mirror rippled, and his cock pushed through like a clear edition of a gloryhole. Hungry to play, to touch, Mary took his cock into her hand. Her tongue teasing and licking the crown made his eyes pop open in time to watch her take all of him into her mouth. His cock bumped the back of her throat, and his body twitched. Palms crumbled into fists against the mirror overhead and he bit his lip as she pulled out his length until her lips popped. Locking eyes with him, she rolled her tongue once more over the edge of his crown, and his cock throbbed in reply.

"This is unfair," he whined.

Pulling slowly off his cock, tongue wiggling firmly against the underside, her lips popped once more before meeting his gaze. "Unfair. This time only your cock came through."

"Tell me I'm just dreaming about a gloryhole with the woman haunting my dreams." He weighed her expression before letting his eyes dip down and back up her naked body as she knelt in a pool of red fabric.

"It's no dream." Her tongue circled the tip of his cock, and he inhaled swiftly. "Does it feel real?"

Flustered, face flushed, CJ confessed, "I haven't been able to orgasm since we met. To be honest, I was afraid that I had made you up and..." He stopped and redirected his intent, "So, if you could lend me a hand?" He arched a brow and smirked. "Perhaps we can help one another out once more."

"Another round of the little death, then?" Mary ran her tongue across his cock's belly from hilt to tip.

"I will give you as many deaths as you please," he cooed, pressing himself against the magical glass barrier that separated them.

Mary's heart fluttered, her eyes locked with his as she took him into her mouth once more, slow and agonizing. *Payback for how slow he teased me last time.* He was swollen and hard; the corners of her mouth ached from the thick girth of his cock. *Oh, to think he gave this to me once before.* Again, he bumped the back of her throat, and she shook her head. A moaned escaped him, tilting his head back, enjoying the heat of her mouth. *Slow. I want him to teeter as I agonize and haunt him.* She rode her lips slowly to the crest, only to slide back to repeat the motion.

Each deep-throated wiggle made him moan louder as his cock throbbed.

"So close," he breathed.

Mary's hand slid down her abdomen between her straddled thighs. Dipping her fingers in and out, she slurped and pumped his staff. Rolling a finger over her pink bud, she moaned, and he thudded against the glass as if bucking from the wave of pleasure her voice brought. As her finger circled her clit, slick and ever faster, she started to peak. Another lustful moan erupted from her as she too bucked, pulling his cock deeper between her lips. Hollowing her cheeks, she pressed forward until the barrier allowed him no deeper. His cock throbbed, jerking once before the heat of his cum filled her mouth, and she swallowed. CJ tilted his head back, moaning as her tongue wiggled and suckled; she swallowed each spurt as she dipped her fingers within herself. She teased him, agonizing as she continued to play by licking his length until he banged on the glass.

"No more," he pleaded between pants.

Releasing him, she wiped her mouth, and a smile crossed her face. "Begging me to stop?"

"Come out," he demanded.

A frowned soured her mood. "I'm trapped," she announced.

"How can you leave?" CJ pushed against the glass. "Is this ... magic? A curse?" He stepped back, looking the mirror over, and when he pushed back, not even his cock could cross the barrier again. "How did you get there in the first place?"

"I don't know." She stood and turned away from him. "If I knew, I wouldn't still be here."

"Tell me, are you visiting me through the mirrors from your room? Where do you live? Can I come to you?" CJ leaned hard against the mirror, his breath fogging the barrier once more. "I want to visit you again, if you'll allow me."

"I ... don't know where I am. This strange place has no end to darkness or mirrors." She dipped her legs into her dress, tugging it up on her hips. "But I would love more visits from you. Someone who sees me as a woman and not a phantom in the mirror."

"If I call your name, will you appear for me?" She spun to see the hungry expression on his face and her breath caught. "How many times shall I say it? Three? Ten?"

"Five." Mary marched closer and leaned against the barrier, the heat of his body still radiating through. "Call my name five times, no less, no more, and I should appear. I should be able to hear you call for me through a mirror of your choice."

"What if I want to touch you?" He raised a palm to the mirror, and both marveled as it passed through where he had been denied just a moment ago. "Is there a trick to this? Something I must do?"

"I don't understand how or why?" Mary hesitated to touch his arm, but without warning, he quickly grabbed her wrist and pulled until her palm locked with the barrier. "See, I cannot cross. You are the first to do so in all the time I've been here. Perhaps I'm nothing more than a phantom after all. With no body to leave the mirror with."

"I wish you could feel how hard and fast my heart beats when I see you, every time I even think of you." His leaned his forehead on the glass, and she placed her own against the barrier, so they could stare into one another's eyes. "Do you remember how you got here?" He released his grip on her wrist, so he could cup her face. "How can I free you?"

"If I could remember... I wish I knew." Tears welled in her eyes.

"Mary, do you have a last name? Maybe I can search for information, proof of your existence," he offered.

"My name..." The memory broke loose, and for the first time, she remembered. *I have a last name!* "Emrys!"

"As in Merlin?" he mused.

"*O Merlin, do ye love me?*" Mary murmured a quote from "Idylls of the King." Some part of her missing life flooded forward; she had once indulged in old texts and poems about magic and knights in the library's archives. "*Great Master, do ye love me?*"

"*Who are wise in love, love most, say least.*" CJ's reply was quick and concise as his thumb glided over her bottom lip. "*To what request for what strange boon?*"

The room and barrier shuddered, and Mary was quick to shove his hand across the barrier. "Go!" she commanded as his mirror became nothing more than darkness. "Is this what it was like, I wonder." She turned back to the abyss of floating lights and reflections with a heavy sigh. "Is this the tower Merlin was imprisoned within when Vivien lost her temple in the old stories?"

6

The Mortal Dream that Never yet was Mine

CJ

CJ was on a mission. His professor did a double take as he rushed down the steps, following him all the way to his office. CJ stuck his foot out to keep the door from slamming shut. Furrowing his brow, they glared at one another in a mute argument. The plump old man snorted, shoving his glasses up and pushing the door for reassurance. CJ's arm thudded on the wood, and his muscles flexed as he pushed it open a little more, earning a rumbling sound from the older man.

"What is the meaning of this, Mr. Galdur!" erupted the Professor, his face red with the rise of his blood pressure as he defeatedly let CJ enter. "This is rather uncouth of you."

"I need to know more about Merlin," demanded CJ, shutting the door behind him. "You're the only one I know who might be able to point me in the right direction."

"Why the sudden interest, my boy?" Clearing his throat, the professor dropped a stack of folders onto his desk, drumming his fingers on a stack of books as he measured CJ. "I mean, besides the old poems, there's not much else to be taught."

"I mean..." CJ paused, searching his thoughts before speaking again, "Merlin was caught in Vivien's tower, so I need to know if or when he escaped?"

The professor narrowed his eyes before he asked, slowly and calculating, "And what makes you think I know the answer to such a quandary?"

"Well, Professor Gawain, I'm pretty sure besides Old English I and II, you've also taught History on Medieval Times, and let's not forget the Arthurian Legends and Lore courses for the Anthropology Department." CJ smirked as the red in Professor Gawain's face returned. "Surely, of all the professors in this college, you are the most well-versed in this."

"You caught me, but you still didn't answer my question." Flopping into his chair, he opened a drawer to produce two shot glasses and an ancient bottle of liquor. "How about we do this shot for shot. We ask, we answer, and we take a shot."

"Fine." CJ took the freshly poured shot. "It's because I met a girl." He chugged it back, and it burned. "What is this stuff?"

Professor Gawain chuckled, pouring his glass. "It's the Holy Grail!" He took a shot and teased, "Your turn again. What does Merlin have to do with a girl?"

CJ watched him fill his cup and remarked, "She shares the same last name. Wasn't his name Myriddin Emrys?" He took his shot, squinting as it only added to the fire in his gut.

"Yes, it is." Professor Gawain giggled as he threw back a shot and exclaimed, "Do you know the origin of your last name?"

"No." CJ took a seat, inhaling deeply before downing his third round. "Ugh, what is this?"

"The Holy Grail, my son!" Gawain pulled his glasses off and refilled the shot glasses once more. "To Galdur and Emrys finding their way back once more!" he cheered, raising the glass high to CJ before sucking it back. "Where did you meet this girl?"

CJ covered his mouth and mumbled through his hand, "In a mirror in the closet." A look of surprise struck his face as he met Gawain's shiny-eyed glare. "What did you put in my glass?"

"Drink first," demanded Gawain. "Go on!" Swallowing, CJ didn't break his stare as he took another shot. "I told you, the Holy Grail. You're wasting questions on the same answers, Chadwick J. Galdur." Another round of shots and refilling of glasses followed. "Tell me, does she cross the barrier or do you? This is vital, so answer in earnest."

As if it were belch rolling to the surface, CJ blurted the answer. "I can sometimes cross into the mirror." He covered his mouth and jolted to his feet. "Fuck!" The world tilted, and he sat back down. "What did—" CJ stopped, his mind reeling as he calmed just enough to think of a more profitable question. "Who are you, really?"

"Ah, now we're asking the right questions, but you need to drink before I can reply." Gawain slid the glass over.

"R-Right. Drink. We ask, we answer, and we inebriate." Reluctantly, CJ drank it.

"I am Gawain!" he announced; laughter filled the room as his cheeks were rosy with liquor. "Knight of the Round Table, King-Consort to Queen Florie of Escavalon in the Fairylands, Finder of Vivien's tower and the last quest of Merlin!" Another shot down, and he exhaled. "Do you love her?"

"Yes," CJ didn't flinch at his own reply. "It's why I need to know how to get her out of there. Do you know how to get Mary out of the mirror?" CJ poured both shots this time, taking his down and slamming the cup.

"The great proof of your love," Gawain answered. "It's as simple as that." He tried to pour more, but the bottle was rendered empty now. "Shoot, she's decided we've had enough." He motioned to the shot. "Did you want it?"

The buzz came on strong and hard, but there was a warming sense of elation as CJ snarked, "You didn't drink."

Cackling erupted from Gawain, and he took the last shot. He added, "We should do this again!"

"I don't know, Professor." CJ slurred his words as he wobbled to his feet. "I'm done drinking with you. When I sober up, we need to talk."

"You should get with Timmy. He might know more." He put the items back into the drawer. "Besides, I can't believe you can stand."

"I need to get home." CJ stumbled out of the office and called Chelsea. "Chelsea, you owe me. Come and get me, bitch."

"Are you, are you drunk?" Chelsea sounded breathless. "Where are you?"

"English hallway?" CJ staggered into the hall, holding his throbbing head as he weaved his way to the bathroom. "I'm in the first-floor men's bathroom." He hung up as she shrieked something. *As many times I've been her chauffeur, she can at least return the favor for once.*

He pushed through the bathroom doors and made his way to the middle sink. He leaned on the counter and wrenched the faucet on; desperately, he splashed cool water on his face and body. Sweat poured over him as his whole body vibrated with the aftermath of the strange liquor. Frustration fueled him.

I don't want to go to the damn gala with Chelsea, he confessed to himself at last. *I don't even love her.* He was quick to unbutton and pull off his shirt as his body temperature continued to rise. *Is it the alcohol, or am I burning a fever?* Shaking his head, he looked into the mirror. Biting a lip, he searched beyond him, hoping to see a flash of lips or red or anything from the world he had slid into twice now.

Heaving a heavy sigh, he placed a hand against the glass. "I'm going to figure this out, Mary." He scoffed to himself, shaking his head as the world tilted and wobbled. "Damn, this shit is strong."

He tried another round of splashing, struggling to knock the heat down and sober up. He was astonished at how, despite the heat in his core, he didn't feel sick or even the slightest sense of nausea. Cursing Gawain under his breath didn't do anything to relieve his throbbing skull.

When I asked him who he was... Squinting at his reflection, a wave of confusion baffled him. *Did he say he was a Knight of the Round Table? As in the Knight Gawain in the stories?* Shaking his head, he tried recalling the information only to find the moment fading as if it was a fleeting memory. *I'm never drinking the Holy Grail ever again.*

"What the hell is wrong with me?" CJ turned the water off. *If I call her, would she...* "Mary Emrys, Mary Emrys." His heart fluttered. *Is it okay to summon her here and now?*

The door slammed open, and he spun to see Chelsea march in with a look of pure rage written across her face. "Why is your shirt off?" She came closer and made a disgusted face. "And why are you sweaty and smell of booze?"

"I drank the Holy Grail with the Knight Gawain," he mused, still feeling he could tell no lies.

"What did you drink?" Chelsea crossed her arms and corrected him. "You mean Professor Gawain?"

"Holy Grail. The knight and I took turns taking shots," he giggled. *I sound like a crazy person, but it's the truth, isn't it? That really just happened!*

"Why would you drink with that fat fuck?" she snarled.

"Hey, he's a king-consort to a queen fairy. And a nice guy," CJ slurred, the Holy Grail still rolling the words out without warning. "Not like you understand that there's more to life than your reputation."

"Look, we need to get you home. You need to forget everything that just happened and get back to ... normal." She grabbed his shirt and shoved it into his chest. "Put on your shirt."

"No," he replied. "I'm hot."

"God, what a big ego you have," she retorted.

"Wow. You're so shallow." Blinking, CJ snorted. "No, like I'm overheating. Why are you so vain? Can't a person express they have a fever using the word *HOT*," he enunciated awkwardly.

Chelsea huffed and rolled her eyes. "Just put your shirt on."

"No," he insisted. "I'm HOT," he repeated.

"Fine." A smile twisted her lips, and she shoved him against the counter, his back to the mirror. "How about..." she spoke slowly as she unbuckled his belt and unfastened his pants, "we have a little fun?"

"No," he said harshly, gripping her wrist to stop her. "No means no, CHEL-SEA," he slurred, wobbling.

"Oh, come on, CJ. Why call me out here?" The anger shifted to sultry in her face and voice, making him flinch. "I know you like the idea of fucking in public. You're already undressed. Why else would you call me?"

"Because I needed a ride?" he answered, regretting having made the call.

Chelsea ran her hands up the ripples of his torso until she hooked them behind his neck. "Come on, baby. I've always wanted to fuck someone in the men's bathroom."

Dryly, he echoed, "*Someone?*" Squinting his eyes, he hooked a finger and pulled her turtleneck down to reveal a fresh hickey. "Maybe you should ask whoever left these to help you fulfill that wish. Jason, perhaps?"

Clapping a hand over it, she shoved away and hissed, "And who left the scratches on your back, huh?"

"Mary Emrys," he spoke without hesitation and bit his tongue. *I wasn't going to confess, but the alcohol is still forcing answers out of me. I mean, I thought I was slipped something, not that I cheated on her. Wait. Let's be honest here. We broke up a month before that anyway, or did she forget? I already knew she was sleeping around on me before the hazing.*

"Oh, yeah? Jason's old fling, huh?" Chelsea puffed herself up. "So, you'd rather be with leftovers who dropped out than with someone like myself."

"Wait, you know who she is?" CJ's chest ached and his heart raced. *This is the answer I need! Do Chelsea and Jason know something? Did they know Mary when she was... was...*

"Fuck me and I might tell you more?" Sucking on a cheek, her eyes dropped to the tightness in his pants. "I mean, I should at least get one more round before we end this, no?"

"Bitch, my dick isn't a merry-go-round ride," he retorted.

"So, it's her and not me now?" The scowl returned, and she marched away, crossing her arms as she spun to face him and reprimand him again. "Huh? Some bitch that you're not man enough to bring around or openly date? As I see it, you want your cake and eat it too!"

"Her name is Mary!" Every nerve in his body tightened, and he couldn't contain it anymore. *If we're going to air my dirty laundry, she's got more, and I'm done dealing with debutant bullshit.* "Since we're being so honest. We broke up months ago because you were cheating on me, and now you call me out. I texted you the week you didn't pick up or reply that this was over. Since then, you seem to be pretending we're still a thing. It's over, Chelsea. It's been over for weeks!"

Chelsea cocked her arm back, ready to slap him as she came marching back. CJ gripped the counter with his hands, white-knuckled and ready to take the hit. Warm hands glided over his shoulders, and Chelsea stopped, stumbling back. She pointed, words lost, as she backed away toward the door. CJ glanced down, and relief filled him as he recognized Mary's arms.

"He's mine now!" Mary's voice sounded ominous as it resonated through the mirrors all at once.

Chelsea released a blood-curdling scream and rushed out, shrieking like a banshee. Heaving a sigh, CJ tilted his head back to see her hovering over him. Her eyes were solid black for a moment before she blinked and looked down at him in surprise.

"Am I..." She pushed against the glass and managed to pull herself out of the mirror a little further. "Am I coming out of the mirror? Oh my God, I'm out! I'm coming out, but I'm stuck," she grunted.

CJ turned to get a better view. "I think so?" Her head, shoulders, and breasts were free as she pushed and wiggled. "Are you stuck?"

She reached for him, and he grabbed her arms. "Ready?" With a nod, he tugged her, but she didn't move, and the mirror wouldn't bend or give. "I think that's as far as you're going to get. Maybe it's like the other day when I couldn't get all of me through the mirror like I had that first time."

Her face became distraught. Tears were falling ever faster, and she began to panic. CJ's heart was breaking. *There must be a way to free her from the mirror.*

7

Have Ye Found Your Voice

MARY

This can't be it. Mary's thoughts spiraled around the possibility of traversing back into the real world. Panic filled her as she wondered, *Will I be denied fully escaping the abyss? Why even let me do this much if I can't get any farther?* CJ had left her arms aching, but neither of them could make the mirror bend or budge. He rushed over to lock the bathroom door.

"In case someone comes by," he explained as his eyes dipped to her breasts and his eyebrows flicked high, "and sees what I see."

His words earned a laugh, despite her tears. "You unzipped my dress, and I can't..." she choked on her words as her panic broke. Sniffling, she said, "It slipped off when I rushed forward to save you from... from... Chelsea." The name rolled from her memory, and she began wiping the tears from her face. "I think ... I know her," she said, unsure of the reason behind it.

"Yeah, I was a little surprised too." He squeezed between two sinks to get closer to where she protruded from the glass. "Apparently, she's banging your ex-boyfriend, Jason?"

"Jason." CJ's hands slid across the glass before tickling her ribs where the mirror had stopped her. "Jason dumped me before the gala, but I don't remember what happened after that." She giggled as fingers glided up her ribs. "Stop, that tickles."

"Well, you stopped crying, which matters more," he murmured as he continued gliding his hands up her torso to cup and grope her breasts. "Does this tickle?" He blew across her nipple, and the heat of his breath made it rise slightly.

"Y-yes." She palmed his forehead but failed to shove him back. "What on earth do you think you're doing?"

"Having some fun with the woman I love." He wrapped his lips around her nipple and suckled long and hard.

A gasp and shriek escaped her. "CJ!" Pushing on his shoulders, she couldn't move him as his tongue flicked and circled. "Oh, this isn't fair!"

His lips popped off her breast, and he smirked up at her. "Why is that? I mean, I owe you from last time." He blew circles around the other nipple and added, "This seems like the perfect time to return the gesture."

"B-b-b-but my hands!" she exclaimed as he took the nipple into his mouth, repeating the motion before releasing her once more.

"Yes? What about your hands?" He arched his brow playfully.

"They're out there," she announced.

"And?" He returned to the other nipple, licking and kissing it passionately.

"I can't get off," she said frustrated.

Moving to the other breast, he replied, "Then this should help for when you can."

Hot lips kissed her other nipple. Hissing as she sucked air between her teeth, his playfulness made her loins ache with desire. From the angle she hung out of the mirror, it was impossible to twist or turn to escape his onslaught. Teeth nibbled at her, and she shrieked once more. At last, she gripped the hair on the back of his head, forcing him to tilt his face up and look her in the eyes. His grin sent goosebumps over her. His tongue snaked out of his lips, and the tip lapped at her nipple. She jerked him back out of reach, and he smirked.

Sucking on a cheek, she warned, "Gentle..."

On the other side of the mirror, her body was heating up and growing wet. Everything throbbed with sexual desire to be touched, licked, and fucked. His hands massaged her breast in anticipation.

"Are you sure you want gentle?" he teased.

"I command you to be gentle," she announced.

"Yes, mistress." He narrowed his eyes.

Slowly, she guided him back to her breast as he lapped out for the nipple with his tongue. She kept him too far to suckle or nibble just yet. His eyes remained fixated on her as the tip of his tongue toyed with the erect nipple. *He sends my body into a frenzy at just a glance. How I wish he was licking my clit this way.* Leading him closer, he gave her breast gentle kisses and sucked softly. Another wave of arousal rolled through and pimpled her skin.

A little closer, he tried to nibble, but she jerked him back again. "I said *gentle*."

"Forgive me, mistress," he muttered as his pants tightened.

"Again, do it right," she demanded, leading him to the other breast.

She hummed as the hot velvet of his tongue ran across her areola before circling her nipple. She pulled him closer, her fingers still interlocked with tresses of his hair as his lips wrapped around her nipple. She moaned as the pleasure made her body buzz. Slowly teasing her, he began to suck and flick. Her body flinched; her loins throbbed with the rise of wanting to go further.

Oh, how I want him to fuck me right now. She bit her lip, moaning as she pressed him harder into her breast.

He suckled harder, deeper, yet slow and agonizing with unpredictable taps and strokes of his tongue. His hand massaged her other breast as his mouth remained latched to her. Taking the other nipple between a finger and thumb, he pinched and tugged. She gasped and whimpered. Wiggling her hips, all she could do was close her thighs tight together in a failed attempt to satisfy the aching desire that lay out of reach. A warm trickle snaked down a leg—her body signaling it was ready and wet for what it anticipated to happen next. Teeth teased her once more, and she shrieked. Releasing her grip on him, she pushed on the mirror in hopes of moving further out—still nothing, not even a millimeter.

CJ moaned into her soft flesh, and her heart thudded fast and hard. *I want to come so badly. If I could just play with myself. I have never wanted a dick inside me so desperately in my life. What the hell!* His actions evolved, becoming rougher and more tantalizing. In reflex, she jerked her legs, knees knocking into the mirror and unable to push him away once more as he swapped breasts once again. He kissed and licked her breasts as if he were making out with them, and it drove her wild.

The sound of a zipper brought her attention elsewhere as he pulled free his hardened length. *I'm not the only one who wants to fully fuck.* He moaned into her breast once more as he stroked his cock. Pulling away, his free hand slid over her collarbone and gripped her neck. She stiffened as he cast a dangerous glare.

"I want to fuck you so bad right now," he confessed.

"I'm so wet and ready." His fingers tightened as he hummed, precum dripping from the tip of his dick. "I want to bend over for you so badly."

"Keep talking." His hand let go, massaging a breast again. "I'm almost ... there," he panted.

Licking her teeth, she cooed, "Are you going to be a good boy and cum for me."

"Yes, mistress," he hissed and grunted, edging closer to a climax.

"Next time, I want that dirty mouth licking my pussy," she confessed.

"Yes, mistress," another grunt as he squeezed her breast tight.

She moaned, eyes dropping to watch him stroke himself faster. "I want to watch you cum."

"I'll cum for you," he reassured breathlessly.

"You better if you want this again..." She pulled the hand off her breast and wrapped her lips around two of his fingers.

A moan escaped him as she suckled on them, wiggling her tongue against them. "Fuck me," he muttered.

She deep throated them, fingertips knocking on the back of her throat. His body went taut and flinched. Her eyes stayed on his stroking until, at last, a stream of cum shot against the mirror. Three more spurts followed as he grunted. His breathing was loud and heavy as he pulled his fingers free from her lips with a pop. They searched one another's expression until their eyes opened in alarm. Mary was moving!

"Shit, you're sliding back in," he interjected.

Panic washed over her. Pushing her hands against the mirror only made them sink in, and she was unable to pull them back out. The abyss started to swallow her back in—slowly but frighteningly picking up speed. Her breasts were sinking into the mirror, and CJ cupped her face. Their lips locked, and he deepened the kiss. The pressure behind it sent her heart aflutter. He kissed her cheek and neck before at last whispering in her ear.

"I promise, I will find a way to get you out of there." With that, he suckled hard and long on her neck.

"Please help me," she said with a quavering voice as her anxiety tightened in her throat.

"I will." He kissed her lips once more before the mirror stole her away.

8

Ride, Ride, and Scream Until Ye Wake

CJ

CJ drummed his fingers on the steering wheel. In the dark garage, his mind just kept spinning in circles. He couldn't get the look of Mary's fearful expression out of his memory. When he lost her in the mirror and failed to call her out again, he had felt dread like no other. After cleaning up his mess, he had raced back to Gawain's classroom to find him gone. He called Chelsea, but she refused to acknowledge what had happened. She acted like he had never asked her to come get him, pretending she didn't see a naked woman in the form of an old friend crawl out of the mirror. More unnerving was that no one seemed to care Mary had gone missing.

Scoffing, he pulled out his cell phone. He scrolled through the history, needing to see it again for reassurance. He confirmed he indeed had called her earlier today. *Is she playing dumb or is there some other magic unfolding here? Could it be people aren't supposed to remember seeing her in the mirror?* He flipped through his texts and paused over his last message from Timmy, fellow frat brother and part-time bellhop out of New Jersey.

[Timmah: Who the hell is Mary?]

CJ's eyes searched the air as he thought for a moment. *He was the one that planned my hazing. Plus, he's majoring in magic and occult history. Maybe he did something or at least knows something I can do to help her.*

[CJ: The girl I met in the closet when you asshats hazed me.]

Waiting, he could see the message flip to "read"; a reply was being actively written.

[Timmah: So, in the closet you met someone named Mary? Did Jason put a girl in there? I told him that was a dick move since you're dating Chelsea. Sorry I wasn't there to supervise.]

[CJ: I broke up with Chelsea months ago. Jason knows that. He was part of the reason why. No, they didn't put a girl in there.]

He waited a moment, but no reply came, so he pressed further.

[CJ: Look. Something weird happened. Aren't you majoring in occult and magic?]

[Timmah: Did they slip acid in your drink?]

[CJ: No.]

[Timmah: Wait, which closet?]

[CJ: The one next to the basement door, under the stairs.]

The phone started to ring.

"You met Bloody Mary?" Timmy blurted as CJ answered.

"How'd you know?" CJ swallowed.

"I bought the mirror because it belonged to someone who got sucked in or was rumored to fall into it." Clearing his throat, Timmy lowered his voice. "So, did you find out who she is? How long has she been stuck in there?"

"Well, that's the weird part." Leaning back into the driver seat, he sat in his driveway, wondering how to even start. *How do I explain something I still can't understand?* "It's Jason's ex-girlfriend."

"The one who went missing?" Timmy seemed alarmed. "Are you sure?"

"Yeah, I mean, Chelsea saw her the last time she appeared," answered CJ as he furrowed his brow. "But now, she acts like it never happened. Mary said they were friends, so it seems—"

"Wait. How many times have you seen her?" CJ could hear Timmy shuffling through a desk drawer. "She keeps reappearing for you. How many times?"

"Um, three times, I think?" CJ's face heated from the memories.

"Just an apparition in the mirror who you can talk to?" The drawer slammed, and a chair squeaked as Timmy called out to someone. "You two stay here, I have to head back to campus."

"Not like I can go far without her anyway," a familiar male voice grumbled.

"Is that Mark?" asked CJ. "Where the hell has he been?"

"Long story." Timmy circled back and pressured for an answer. "Can you communicate with her?"

"About that, I, um..." CJ choked, coughing a few times before blurting his confession, "I fucked her the first time."

"You what?" The phone fell silent for a long while. "And what about the other times?" Timmy asked slowly and calculating.

"We talk and touch and, well, cross in or out of the mirror but only partially." CJ groaned and added, "I sound like a lunatic."

"No, you don't," Timmy reassured him. "So have you been visiting the mirror in the closet to look for her?"

"No." CJ was offended at the idea. "I call her name five times, and she appears in a mirror sometimes."

There was silence again as the sound of a car started. He couldn't make out the conversation; clearly, Timmy's hand was over the phone. A woman's voice fussed, and before long, another door shut and the engine revved. The familiar delayed connection of a handsfree system caught the last bit clearly.

"Fine, but it's dangerous," relented Timmy.

CJ's nerves tightened, and he added, "Look, I don't know what is happening, but it's crazy and honestly..." CJ shuddered as Mary's face came to mind once more. "I want to help her escape that place."

"Okay, if you're willing, I might be able to pull this together." Timmy sighed, and after another long pause, he started to divulge information. "The mirror in the closet is the one Jason pushed her into."

"Jason?" Scoffing, CJ retorted, "You make it sound as if Jason purposely put her in that mirror." The long pause that followed made his stomach twist. "C'mon, Tim. Someone can't just curse someone into the mirror."

"They can... and have." Timmy inhaled deeply. "How much do you know about Merlin and his mistress, Vivien?"

"Gawain already talked to me about that," mumbled CJ.

"Oh. So, he actually revealed—" Timmy stopped and changed what he intended to say. "Look, CJ, Jason isn't who and what you think he is."

"He's a scumbag," CJ announced flatly.

"Agreed, but we're talking about something not ... normal ... or even human," Timmy suggested.

"What part of this conversation is fucking normal," announced CJ.

"What if I told you he was a changeling?" Timmy offered. "Do you know what that is?"

CJ struggled for words before he blurted, "As in a child swapping fairy?"

"See, for an English major, you know your stuff," commended Timmy. "Sometimes it happens as a newborn, and the stronger ones can completely replace teenagers in most cases. But the ones you have to watch out for are those who steal the likeness of grown-ass people, including owning their life, not just their looks."

"Jason's a changeling?" CJ furrowed his brown, struggling to process the idea.

"And not any changeling," warned Timmy. "He can hide a person anywhere. Normally, they just misplace you in our world or send you to live out your days in the fairy realm where you turn fae and at least gain some powers, but he's a dark changeling." Tim hesitated as if trying to put the words together. "As crazy as this may sound, they can put people into a dark realm, a mirror realm, where they age more slowly and can watch the outside realm from windows or mirrors. On occasion, if there's magic or a strong enough connection, they can contact someone on the outside, but it's rare."

CJ listened, hand over his mouth. *Magic? Realms? Fae? Jason's a fucking changeling? What the hell is happening here? Did Professor Gawain slip me LSD?*

"Which brings me back to Merlin and Vivien." Timmy cleared his throat.

"What does that have to do with them?" CJ shook his head and spoke louder, "What does any of this have to do with me?"

"Vivien used the magic from a dark changeling to trap Merlin in the tower," declared Timmy. "Mary, the one in the mirror who Jason hid away, her last name is Emrys. The same as Merlin." Timmy spoke slowly and seriously. "And then we have Vivien Galdur."

"Mary is Merlin, and I'm..." CJ leaned back in the driver seat, rubbing his forehead.

"Right, so here's where it really gets weird..." Timmy sounded like he was tiptoeing now with the information.

"What a damn minute," growled CJ. "How do you know all of this shit about me, Jason, fucking Bloody Mary?"

There was a long hush before Timmy sighed and relented, "You wouldn't even believe me if I told you."

"Try me," CJ pressed. "I want answers for it all."

"Fine. Listen, if you do love her, there's a chance we can break her out, but..." Timmy groaned as if pained. "I like to fuck with people and trick them, but not completely destroy lives. In the end, I just want some good entertainment. I mean, I can't help it. It's in my nature."

"What's the problem?" demanded CJ. "Spit it out already."

"You need to figure out how to get into the mirror realm. Not just your dick, but all of you. It's going to be a dangerous move," Timmy forewarned.

"Yeah, because I can get stuck in there," CJ confirmed.

"No, because there is ancient magic teamed with fae magic. Jason has some control just as Vivien did. Possibly, you do too?" Timmy seemed unsure. "And she must love you back. The confession goes both ways, and I don't know how much that old adage of true love plays into this. I'm completely guessing, CJ."

"There has to be a way to make sure we can leave there once we reach her," CJ insisted.

"The mirror in the closet is the original." Timmy hummed in thought, working out the possibilities in his mind. He announced, "I suspect it was a magical heirloom when I first found it. To think, it could be the portal Vivien used and kept in the forest. Anyway, if you find that specific mirror, you can pull her out. Maybe if I can get there in time, I can lend you a hand with the magic. If Jason comes for you, play dumb—you know nothing. If he gets even a hint or suspicion that you know he's not human, he'll slit your throat."

"In that case, I'm counting on you." CJ ended the call. *I've got a plan, but I need to think this through.*

9

Know Ye the Stranger Woman

MARY

Panting, Mary's body buzzed with elation despite the overwhelming feeling of crushing dread. She could still feel the cold of the mirror swallowing her, overshadowing the heat of the moment. *The way he clung to me when he realized it was taking me back...* The look on his face only added to the pang in her chest. *I'm not the only one feeling broken that I couldn't completely crossover.*

Everywhere his lips and tongue had teased left behind heat not even the cold mirror could snuff out, driving her arousal to an aching like no other. *I don't want to cry anymore. Please, just take this pain away. Don't let the pleasure still haunting me be extinguished.* Laying back on the floor in the darkness, her hands slid between her thighs. *I'll cling onto what good vibes I have in this shit moment.* Mirrors twinkled all around like flickering candles.

I want to feel... A finger slid between the swollen folds of her pussy, rubbing across the slick opening. *...alive!* Her breath caught and her touch revived what he had set in motion. With ease, her finger slipped inside, hot and wet; she ached with desire. *Oh, how I wish I could feel his cock inside me again. I want him to fuck me.* Stroking in and out, her pussy tightened on her fingers, and she whimpered in frustration.

Eyes shut tight, she focused on recalling those first moments with CJ—the heat of his body and torso caught between her thighs. The lingering memories made her arch as she bit her lip. Her finger glided out and up to circle her clit. A moan escaped her as her body tensed, the tingling of her arousal increasing. Skin pimpled in anticipation and groping her own breast, she clung to the feeling of his tongue on her nipples.

So close... Her fingers stroked in and out once more. She imagined the heat of his hands running up her legs, lips on her own, and even his voice as he—

Mary, Mary. CJ's voice filled her ears.

Again, she returned to circling her pink jewel. "Call my name again," she pleaded.

Mary... Louder, she heard the voice and a fist pounding on a mirror, lost in the sea of the abyss. *Mary... cum...* His voice faded as she peaked.

Her muscles tightened as she sat up, sucking in air, eyes wide open from the exhilaration of the violent release. Fingers dove inside to feel how her pussy tightened in her orgasm. At last, she cried out as she egged the orgasm on until she peaked higher, squirting from the stimulus of it all. Breathlessly, she came to a stop and looked all around at the twinkling of glass in the silent space. Creasing her forehead, she finally gathered the thoughts to express the sudden confusion.

"It's quiet." The unease tightened in her chest as a chill crossed her body, skin dimpling once more. "Since the moment I woke up here, it's never been this quiet." She gathered her dress and slipped it on, tugging it up as she glanced around. "Why are all the mirrors so far away and no one's calling my name?" Her heart began racing, the dryness in her mouth adding to her building fear. "Does that mean I can't even hear CJ?"

"That's right," a familiar male voice replied within the darkness. "He can't call you, you can't hear him, and I can make this permanent if you don't behave, Mary."

Chills snaked up her spine, bristling the hairs on her arms. "Jason."

He stepped out from behind an old, wooden-framed mirror in the distance, much like the one she recalled seeing CJ in that first time. "What are you doing here?" Her stomach knotted. "You did this to me, didn't you?"

"I had a reputation to keep, and if you would have stayed home from the gala that night and not caused a fucking scene..." he snarled as his eyes went solid black and his skin sparkled like shimmering water. "It's not easy for my kind to blend in, and had I known you were a cambion—"

"A what?" she chirped, confused. "A cambion? What in the hell is that?"

"Don't be coy with me." He snorted in frustration, agitated as he ran a hand through his hair. "I thought you were human, and ever since I slept with you I just can't—"

"Fuck you!" She gave him a baffled expression and exclaimed, "I'm human! You're the fucking creature who threw me into a mirror-filled hell hole!"

Jason gave a disgusted expression, curling his lip to reveal a fang. "Are you telling me you don't even know what you are? *A chrebair chuilig*. You flea-ridden woodcock." He muttered something in another language before sneering at Mary once again. "You're an insult to your lineage."

"What the fuck..." Mary was shocked over the insult to injury. "I'm trapped here, and you show up just to patronize me? Why? Because you can?"

Snorting, he closed the gap between them in an instant; she had no time to react until it was too late. His fingers wrapped tightly around her throat, and his soulless eyes burned away her anger until fear sent her body trembling. She could barely keep her toes on the ground as she pulled at his arm. *This is it; I'm dying here.* Tears welled in her eyes, and she let her arms fall to her sides in defeat. Closing her eyes tight, she thought bitterly, *At least I'll leave here if I die.*

He gave another disgusted hiss as he dropped her to the floor. "Please, I don't have enough clout to stand trial if I kill you, even if you're only cambion. They'd strip me of my title and far worse."

Coughing and sputtering, she croaked, "What the hell is a cambion?"

Exasperated, he knelt before her and held her chin, forcing her to meet his gaze. "I suppose I owe you this much. Half human, half incubus, or in this case, succubus." Releasing her, he paced away toward that singular and specific antique mirror. "Surely, an old English geek like yourself recalls tales of Merlin being a cambion? Granted, there are no books here to keep you entertained."

She swallowed hard and took a deep breath. Mary demanded, "Why have you come here?"

"To warn you." He turned back to face her, running his fingers through his hair again. "Stop reaching out to CJ ... or else."

"Or else what?" Mary threw out her arms. "You'll throw him in here?"

Jason scoffed, laughing before he answered, "And give you a chance to gain power, so you both can break out of here? I think not." He ran a finger across his throat. "I'll kill your human fuck boy in a heartbeat."

Rage and fear fought against one another inside her for a fleeting moment before the anger drove her to shout. "And what if you're wrong about him too?"

"Excuse me?" Jason furrowed his brow.

"What if your wrong?" Mary pulled herself to her feet, tugging the dress up before balling her fists at her sides. She yelled, "He's not human either!"

Rage was written on his face, his fangs gritting.

"If you think I reached out to him, you're wrong!" *Shit, what am I doing? Won't this put a target on CJ?* Biting her lip, she didn't want to spin it further. "Whatever you are, you're shit at recognizing others, so be sure before you act." *That's it, plant enough self-doubt and just maybe...* "Whatever the hell you are, you can't be that powerful if me fucking another guy riles you up."

Again, he was at her throat. "Listen, wench, pissing off a dark changeling is a dangerous matter." Letting her go, Jason marched for the mirror. "Fucking succubi and their pheromones that keep their mates coming back. Never again." And with that, he disappeared into the mirror before it faded away into the dark.

10

Who Pounced Her Quarry and Slew It

CJ

CJ paced in his bedroom, mind spiraling with everything Timmy had told him. Some of it made obscure sense, while other answers left him baffled. All he could confidently confirm was he had magic, she had magic, and magic had caused the fiasco of her being trapped in a mirror for years. *I knew Jason was a dick, but shit.*

Glancing down at his phone, he wondered if he should call Timmy again or even his professor to pry further. His stomach turned, and he shook his head at both ideas. *Timmy is on his way back; I can wait. As for the other, I don't think I can handle another round of the Holy Grail.* He marched to the mirror and pounded his fist against it.

"Where are you, Mary?" He searched his own eyes. "Why haven't you heard me? Or replied?"

Pulling off it, he walked away holding his mouth. *Did it somehow end our connection? If so, is there a way to get it back? Is it possible I broke it somehow? Or does she not want to see me?* He twisted, crossing his arms as he stared in frustration at his reflection in the mirror.

"What happened to you, Mary?" A scowl crossed his face, but again, he didn't see the world that once lay just under his reflection and gaze like before. "Why can't I get in or, at the very least, see it?"

Suddenly his reflection smiled and placed its hands on their hips. "What's the matter, CJ?" The deep voice resonated in the mirror. "Did you lose something?"

CJ's heart leapt to his throat, and he struggled to swallow it. He took a few steps back until his legs pressed against his bed. *So, he can pass through the mirrors, but do I let him know I know who he is? No, Timmy said play dumb if he comes after me.*

"It's all a dream," cooed the black-eyed version of himself in the mirror, waving a hand in a grand gesture. "The stress has eaten away at you. Pull yourself together," it reassured.

Are you kidding me? CJ sat on his bed, balling fistfuls of his comforter as he stared wide-eyed. *Magic is a terrifying thing, but how is this any different from how he's manipulated me outside of this?* He could feel a calm starting to take over as his fear dissipated at each suggestion the doppelganger offered to him.

"The gala is a big event, and let's be honest, the hazing ritual went too far," it offered. "Clearly, someone slipped something into your drink. Surely, if you ask Jason, he'll confirm it."

CJ covered his mouth and mumbled, "What the fuck."

"Now, pull yourself together. Chelsea needs you to take her to the gala tonight," it demanded. "Don't disappoint Jason and the fraternity. They need you to make an appearance and keep your shit together." It pounded the mirror with its palms, making CJ flinch. "As for Mary," it warned with a hiss, "forget she ever existed. It's the best for you. Don't you want your life back?"

The mirror shattered into a million pieces. Tiny shards bounced and rained down on the floor, some of them tapping against his shoes. Rage filled CJ. *Who the fuck does he think he is? How is this any different from a jealous, dickhead ex-boyfriend showing up and trashing my room? Fuck this. I'm not scared. I'm not afraid of being cursed into the mirror realm with her if that's how this ends. Before that, I'll make it clear I intend to fight back. Two can play at the game of manipulation. Let's make him let his guard down.*

A grin flashed across his face as he stood. Glass crunched under his shoes as he went to the closet to pull out the tuxedo he had intended to wear. *You want me at the gala, Jason? Fine. But you're going to regret it.*

[CJ: Hey Jason. Did you ever figure out if someone slipped something in my drink?]

[FratBoss: Oh! Hey man! You feeling, ok? Yea, we found out who did it and reported him. You still coming to the gala?]

Ha! CJ marched for the bathroom. *Eager to see if you convinced me? Does this mean you can't force anyone to do your bidding? Or am I somehow immune?*

[CJ: In that case, I'm relieved.]

[FratBoss: Me too. So, the gala...?]

[CJ: I'll let Chelsea know I'll pick her up. Getting ready. You said you had some plans for after the gala?]

[FratBoss: Yea. I'll explain when you get there. It's an after-party celebration at our frat house and Chelsea's sorority is joining.]

CJ froze. *That's a little weird. Why keep that secret?* Every nerve tightened as he started the shower and waited for the hot water. *Something's not right.*

[CJ: Hey Tim. What's your ETA?]

[Timmah: Uh, well Mark and his girl came so a few hours out. Meet at the gala?]

[CJ: Ok. What does our fraternity and Chelsea's sorority have in common?]

[Timmah: Huh? That's rather specific.]

[CJ: Jason's up to something. Not sure where I fall but I got a bad feeling about tonight.]

[Timmah: I'll make some calls.]

Tossing his phone on the vanity, he shed his clothes and slid under the water. Heat and steam enveloped him, but his mind couldn't let go of thoughts of Mary. Licking his lips, the taste of her skin and the soft warmth of her breasts came rushing back. A groan rolled from him, starting deep in his gut before he let it audibly escape his lips. His hand slipped down his abdomen and he started to stroke his cock slow and steady. He grew stiffer with each round, the tingling and arousal growing.

"Mary..." Each tug grew firmer as he came to a full hard-on. "Mary..." He muttered with eyes shut as streams of water raced down his body. "Mary..." A moan escaped as he curled his toes. "Mary..." Muscles grew taut, and he braced his other arm against the shower wall as he began to peak. "Mary..." he moaned her name, leaning his head back as he came. "Mary..." Her name left his lips like a sigh of relief.

Finishing, his body buzzed from thoughts and memories of her. Drying off, he glanced at the tiny mirror, wondering if she had at least heard or seen him beyond the haze of steam across the glass. The alarm on his phone startled him, and he shut it off. *This is it. The gala. I'll destroy you if it's the last thing I do in the world of the living, Jason.* He pulled on his tuxedo with practiced skill and paused before sliding his tie to his collar.

He caught a look at himself in the mirror and grinned. "Fuck this."

Leaving the tie loose, he unbuttoned the jacket and top buttons on his white shirt. Pulling the cufflinks back out, he tossed them onto the vanity.

Leaning onto the counter, he smirked. "Just you wait, Mary. I'm coming for you."

Marching away, he texted Chelsea.

[CJ: You better be out front when I drive up or I'm not stopping.]

11

Arriving at a Time of Golden Rest

MARY

None of the mirrors were answering to her. She could hear murmurs but nothing as clear as before. *Fuck you, Jason.* Running from one place to the next, the mirrors were just out of reach before shooting far away. Lungs starting to sting, she leaned on her knees as sweat dripped from her chin. *How could he do this to me?* She sunk to her knees and fought back the tears threatening to spill forth.

"That asshole doesn't deserve my despair." She sniffled, wiping her cheek. "I guess it's all up to CJ to rescue me. But I'm just some apparition in a mirror. I heard Jason talk him into believing that I'm just a drug-induced hallucination a moment ago. I mean, that makes more sense than the truth."

More tears fell, and she wiped to no avail to keep them from streaking down the length of her face. *How could I not realize I was sleeping with a monster? And worse, he broke it off with me to go out with my best friend Chelsea. I mean, what is so special about her?*

"Mary..." Her name sounded like a sigh.

"CJ?" One mirror stood out near where she sat. "Come, mirror." Much to her relief, it rushed to her call. "It's CJ, but the mirror is too fogged over. Can you hear me?" She hugged it. "I guess not. He really did cut my ability to communicate."

Looking around, the darkness had lost its beauty—now bare of all sparkling mirrors. The mirror in her arms buzzed with warmth despite the cold enveloping her in the absence of the vibrant magic and candlelight.

"Fuck this." CJ's voice came through clearly.

"CJ!" The mirror wiped clear now, she watched him make himself appear disheveled. "CJ! CAN YOU HEAR ME?" she shrieked into the mirror with no response from him. "Fuck! I can't do anything like this! What's happening?"

"Just you wait, Mary. I'm coming for you." He marched away, leaving her staring in disbelief.

"What does he mean he's coming for me?" Pulling to her feet, the mirror faded to nothing in her hands. "Shit! Where did he go?" She squinted her eyes all around, hoping for a glimmer or any sign. "Come on, there must be another. Something about him keeps breaking through. Come on, CJ, where are you?"

"I hope you're watching," CJ scoffed. "It's going to be quite the show."

A sparkle caught her eye, and she summoned the mirror. "Ah, a rearview mirror!" He was driving as she watched helplessly.

Every nerve tightened as he stopped to let Chelsea slide into the passenger seat. Her eyes glanced at the mirror for a moment before darting away and nudging it off herself. *She knows! Not in a I-saw-a-naked-mirror-ghost-grab-my-boyfriend way but more of a my-ex-bestie-is-watching-me-from-there-guilty way! What the hell are she and Jason planning on doing to CJ?*

Standing up, Mary looked around the abyss and began walking aimlessly like she had done so many times before. "Where was it? I kept shoes on this whole time until CJ came and when I was running a moment ago... Yes!" Carpet, old and torn, lay across the cold, black marble at her feet. "This must lead somewhere."

Swallowing her fear, she held the mirror tight and began to follow the runner. With the images upright, it seemed purposeful, and she presumed it led someplace important. *Where? Why haven't I found it or noticed before?* Pictures of kings, queens, knights, and wizards lay faded. In some places, it looked as if someone had burned holes of ripped out entire entities—at least their faces.

Looking at the mirror in hand, she couldn't hear anything. CJ glanced into it constantly, searching, and she knew it was for her. Inhaling deeply, she held her breath in hopes of keeping her emotions at bay. *I need to trust him. He's figured something out. Now, I need to keep calm and really see this place for the first time.*

Exhaling, she stumbled to a stop. The runner came to an end, and she stood in front of a large room lit by a fireplace. The hearth was massive, something worthy of a castle. The warm, wooden floor was soft to the touch as if well-maintained and waxed. Stacks of books and shelves with jars and more leather-bound tomes filled the three walls. Her heart skipped a beat, fluttering as she took it in.

"Fucking walls! And ... and..." A blood-curdling scream escaped her. "Holy shit!"

She tripped on the carpet, falling back on her rump. In one of the high-backed chairs were two skeletons entangled with one another. She shook as she slid further back, at a loss for words. *What in the hell is this? Some fucking "A Rose for Emily" moment? Who are they? I mean, I suspected someone died here, but I wasn't hoping to fucking find them!*

A log popped in the fireplace, making her yelp before she turned back. "They're gone?" In a blink of an eye, the skeletons had vanished with nothing more than a piece of parchment in their place. "Where the hell am I? What's going on?"

The mirror in her hand dissipated, and she muttered curses under her breath. She sat, staring at the letter, too scared to move or even venture where death had embraced death. *Pull yourself together, Mary. This isn't Jason. It's too much like a dark romance or gothic romance vibe. Clearly, someone else was trapped here, waiting to be found.* Standing up, she whimpered to herself. *But why did it have to be me?*

Tiptoeing to the chair, she kept searching all around. *I swear if something pops out at me, I'm going to start swinging. It's not like I can run away.* The old, thick parchment was too dark to read so far from the fire. Huffing, she wandered closer to the fire, tugging her dress up once more in annoyance. At last, she could read the faint ink scrawled across it.

To our descendants who find themselves caught in my spell. Beware of the dark changeling, for he seeks what I promised and denied him. You see, it was my magic I offered if he could help me ensnare my lover.

My pride and desire have brought an end to the love of my life, and soon after, I shall follow him to the depths of Hell, always there in his shadow for all eternity.

One day, the changeling will try to recreate the spell to syphon the magic. If you find yourself in such a situation, I bid you good luck.

You see, in my foolishness, the only way I made to break the spell is—

Ink had spilled across the page, and the last line only gave the writer's name.

Yours truly,
Vivien Galdur

"Of course, I can't see it." Balling it up, she threw it at the chair. "How fucked up that I have to pay for Merlin's mistress' tower. What kind of dumb luck is this?" she shouted, fists at her sides. "THIS SUCKS!" Her voice echoed throughout the room.

Looking at the other high-backed chair, she sat down. *Oh, to be able to sit in a real chair and have a warm fire.* Her eyelids grew heavy. *So tired.* Pulling her legs onto the chair, she hugged her knees as sleep weighed down on her. *At least I feel safe here. It reminds me of Grandma's house... I can remember being a kid... I remember the dance... it's like I'm a shattered mirror scattered across the floor...*

12

While All the Heathen Lay at Arthur's Feet

CJ

Pushing through the double doors and into the main event ballroom, CJ grimaced. All around were elegant gowns of all colors and types, but he failed to recall that that it was intended to be a masquerade. *No one said anything about wearing a mask. I have a bad feeling about this.* Masked faces halted to face him; his exposed face sent murmurs all around the room. As soon as Chelsea pushed him aside to enter, they all snapped back, resuming what they had been doing.

He gripped her arm, forcing her to stay close to him. "Chelsea."

"I have nothing to say to you." She didn't even attempt to look at him. She wore a mask on her face; moments before in the car, she hadn't even let him know he would need one. "Let me go."

"What's really happening here?" he demanded. "The masks? Mary? Jason and you? What's supposed to happen at this gala with Mary and I being a central part?"

She yanked her arm back, her eyes dark within the mask, and she shoved him back a few steps. "Just play your part." She disappeared in the crowd.

"Fuck me." CJ wandered over to the appetizer table and popped a grape in his mouth. *She didn't even acknowledge how disheveled I look. Not a flinch, sneer, or anything. That means she doesn't care how I look as long as I'm here. Jason, what the hell are you planning to do with me tonight? Is this what they did to Mary? Is it because we are descendants of wizards or something?*

CJ continued to pick at the food in thought. *I mean, this whole thing seems off. The way she's at Jason's every beck and call and the pressure to join his frat house. Was I being manipulated well before Mary became involved? Is there a reason they are trying to do all this while Timmy is away, seeing he's an occult and magic expert?*

Then, he had an epiphany. Patting his pockets, he desperately searched for his cell phone. *Where the fuck is it?* A chill crept up his spine, and he raised his chin to meet Jason's gaze. In his hand, he wiggled CJ's cell phone. Chelsea stood behind him, turning her face away. *She always does that when she feels guilty and can't admit she's done something wrong. So, this is it. He's planning some magical event, and I'm the target. Does that mean everyone here is...*

Scanning the room, the gala seemed to take a dark turn. Baroque music filled the room, and he realized something was off about the dancing couples as they took turns, exchanging partners, and filling the space with tandem coordination straight out of a historical film. *There's no fucking way this many college brats mastered classical ballroom dancing overnight.* His heart pounded hard in his chest and nausea washed over him. *The whole place is in on it, and I'd bet not one of them are human.*

His gaze bounced from mask to mask. He saw irises in yellows and reds, glowing with cat-like pupils. Under them, crimson-painted lips covered their fangs. Looking closer, some even had misshapen ears. Their laughter at his impending doom began to fall on him in this fleeting moment. Rushing back a few steps, he bashed into the table. A three-tier tray of mini quiches toppled over with a loud clatter, sending him running out the door.

I need to escape! Behind him, he heard the rush of footsteps. *It's not just Jason after me!* Thoughts filled his mind. *Where do I even hide or go?* Turning a corner, a group was rounding the opposite end of the hall. He doubled back and took a different hallway. Tugging and pushing on doors, he pleaded, *Come on! One of these ... just one of these should be enough.* At last, a door pushed open, and he stumbled in. His heart stopped.

"Really? The women's restroom?" He turned to lock the door. "Fuck! No lock? What is up with this building!" Spinning, he stared wide-eyed at the frightened expression of his face in the mirror. "The mirror!" He rushed it, palms smacking against it. "If only I could go through it like that time before when no one could find me for a few days. Jason didn't even know where I went, so there's a chance." Looking at his reflection, he steeled himself. "I can do this. If I am a descendant of Vivien, then I can control the mirror world like Jason." Taking a few steps back, he glared at the mirror with new resolve. "Mary Emrys, Mary Emrys, Mary Emrys, Mary Emrys..." He paused, licking his lips before saying it for the fifth and final time. *Please let her or the magic hear me this time.* "Mary Emrys."

The smell of a fire burning met his nose, and he rushed forward. Hands shoved him from behind in his moment of wanting to slow down. *Shit! They found me!* Bracing to smack into the mirror, he tensed and closed his eyes. *Please let me in!* A rush of frigid air washed over him like a curtain before he slammed into a chair and fell to the ground with it. A woman's scream filled the air. He scrambled to his feet in time to see Mark, now translucent, nod and smash the mirror, so it would start to dissipate.

"M-Mark?" he sputtered. "MARK!"

"Closet!" Mark shouted as the last tendrils faded away.

CJ turned to the panting woman who held her chest, no longer able to keep her shrieking going. "M-Mary!"

She rushed to her feet. "CJ? But how? Did Jason…?"

"No." CJ patted himself down a moment as if checking that all of him had made it to the other side. "Where are we?"

"I don't know. Well, you're inside the mirror, but I just found this place," she confessed. "After that first time together, I lost track of my shoes and noticed a carpet. When I followed it, I found … walls," she offered. "Wait, how did you find me?"

"I called your name." CJ marveled over the space and the direction he had come, picking the chair up. "Could you not hear me?"

"No." Mary tugged on her dress. "I suspect it was Jason."

"Fucking Jason," CJ guffawed. "Dark changeling bullshit."

"A what?" Mary marched toward him, poking a finger into his chest. "You know what's happening? I want answers, CJ. Are you the reason why I'm here?"

CJ froze. "I don't even know anymore."

His gaze followed her arm up to her neck to the furrowed brow and scowling lips of red. *Mary is pissed. She has every right to be.* His heart fluttered as he searched her eyes, wondering how much she knew. *Does she know she's a descendant of Merlin? That I'm a descendant of Vivien? Does she know there's something magical and haunting about who we are? The irony of being here in this tower of mirrors like the original cast of some fairy tale. I might be just as obsessed about her as Vivien was over Merlin in the room...*

With a sigh, he pushed her arm down and pulled her into a full embrace. He whispered, "I'm so glad you're okay. I was worried he had done something to you after he cut us off from one another."

The tension released in her body as fingers clutched the back of his shirt, desperate to hold him closer. "Me too," she relented, choking back the sobs. "What is he? Why me? How was I supposed to know I'm some kind of monster."

CJ pulled back. "You? A monster?" He cupped her face, using his thumbs to push the tears away. "No, never," he reassured. *Fucking Jason. What did you say and do to her? Was imprisoning her here not good enough?*

"Jason said I'm a cambion." She abandoned the embrace and turned away. The back of her dress hung open as she pulled it up once more. "I don't know ... how and what," she said, pausing to swallow. "Look, I'm sort of half-blooded succubus or demon."

"Like Merlin. Yes, that makes sense," he consoled her in a soft tone. "Just like your ancestor. It's okay."

"Is it?" she inquired.

"What does it change?" he pressed.

"I'm sorry. If I had known it would cause anyone, especially you, so much distress..." Mary's words faltered, and the muscles in her back tensed.

"Distress?" he questioned, confused. "What kind of distress? I feel fine."

"Well, you know..." She was too afraid to finish and gazed over her shoulder. "The problem with..." She hesitated again. "Down there. Jason and you."

"You lost me." He tilted his head, baffled as he arched a brow. "What do you think you did to me? And Jason?"

"Well, Jason can't get it up since he slept with me, so I assume—"

"Oh, hell, no!" CJ blurted, rubbing his forehead. "Is this why he has you here? Because he's got limp dick? Holy fuck..." The idea blew his mind, and he panicked to reply. "Look, it works perfectly fine without you. Granted..." His face flushed.

"It does?" She straightened her back, ears red with embarrassment and still too ashamed to turn to face him. "Are you sure it works without me?"

"Yes, it does!" he shouted, startling them both. "I mean, thinking about you turns me on, but I don't think that has to do with what you are. It's about how I feel ... about you." His words slowed, his shoulders dropping. *Just confess it. I mean, it seems silly to fall in love at first sight, but who in the hell else will I ever find who can go tit for tat with geeky references? This is worth an eternity of little deaths, and I'll gladly give her my soul if she wishes.* "I love you, Mary. It seems crazy. We barely know each other, but the chemistry and the way you look at me..."

Mary dared to peek over her shoulder at last. "You ... love me?" She asked skeptically. "Are you confessing that you love me? Some woman in the mirror?"

"I do," he confirmed. "I love you. Not an apparition, but the Victorian Era geek who was quick to tell Jason and his paranormal debutants to fuck themselves."

She looked away, once more clutching the front of her dress. "But what if it's all because of what I am? What if your feeling of love is from the demon side of me making you feel that way?"

CJ closed the gap between them, fingers tracing down the divot of her spine. "Then let me show you once more how much I mean it. Surely, you feel it as I do when we make love, when we kiss. Even now, you resist looking me in the eyes, knowing fully well you can't deny it either. Tell me you love me too, Mary."

Mary leaned into him, allowing the dress to slide to the floor. "Show me once more," she demanded. "Make me fall for you one more time, so I can be sure this isn't some delusion. My heart beats so fast thinking of you, and I don't know if it's affection or a false hope I can leave here," she confessed.

"Well, we're both stuck in here," he reassured her. "So, let's see what unfolds in this moment when we have all the time in the world."

13

With Dark Sweet Hints of Some Who Prized Him More

MARY

The heat from his hands glided over her hip and ribs. One hand ascended to grope a breast, the other descended to dive between her thighs. She leaned into the hard planes of his torso as his finger glided over her clit and followed her channel to the weeping door that awaited him. *Is it okay to lose myself to passion? Am I allowed to fall to hard for a man I've only lusted after since the moment he fell into my world?*

His lips kissed at her neck as his finger slipped inside her. She lifted an arm, running her fingers through his hair. Tension and doubts lost hold as pleasure and desire took over. His finger retreated to her pink pearl and began slowly circling, making her loins ache and buzz with arousal. She felt his cock growing hard within his pants as he pressed it between her ass cheeks. He pinched her nipple, and she moaned in reply. He kissed his way up, suckling on her earlobe.

"Sit down in the chair," he demanded, letting her go.

Mary abandoned her dress on the floor and sat on the chair. Nervous, heart racing, she sat with thighs closed as she stared up at the amazing man before her. CJ pulled off the tie and dropped it. After shedding the jacket, he unbuttoned his shirt and tugged to unbuckle his pants. His fierce gaze locked onto her where she sat, naked and swallowed by the high-backed velveteen tufted chair. Swallowing, she watched with arousing anticipation as his shirt fluttered to the ground, and he wiggled out of his pants. Shoes clunked onto the wooden floor, and she found herself shivering at the sight of him. As CJ stroked his hard cock before her, the distance between them seemed agonizing. She marveled over him just as she had done the day she sucked his cock through the mirror.

"Now, I recall someone telling me that next time I'm to..." His gaze shifted, dropping to her thighs. "...lick her pussy."

Mary's face blushed, and she pressed her thighs tight together. "I was just talking dirty to help you," she insisted.

"Look, I take such requests very seriously." He knelt before her, hands hot on her thighs, squeezing them.

"CJ." Her heart fluttered as he pushed her legs apart with a devilish smirk on his face and a sparkle in his hazel eyes.

"Yes, mistress," he murmured, leaning in as his shoulder slid past her knees.

"I don't think I can handle this," she half-laughed.

"You shouldn't demand things you aren't prepared to take responsibility for." The heat of his breath rolled over her pussy, and her back straightened.

"I confess," she blurted.

He paused and looked up as she held her reddened face. "You're the first to ever stop me."

"I've been fingered plenty of times, but…" she choked on her works, legs squeezing him.

"*But?*" he echoed back to her, biting his lip as he arched a brow.

"I've never…" She covered her face and quickly said, "I've never been licked down there!"

CJ laughed a moment, enjoying how her whole body shivered and flushed. "Is that all?"

"Is that all?" she flustered. "This is something I've never experienced, and I don't know if I want to!"

"Oh, trust me. I'm honored to be your first on this one." His grin was wide, and he leaned back on his heels to give her some space, so he could really take in her full reaction. "I don't think I've ever had a woman say no, let alone need to discuss this beforehand." CJ chuckled.

"It's not funny," she pouted, peeking through her fingers. "I don't think I can handle it."

"Look, I'm telling you, you'll love this more than you can imagine." Now his face flushed, and he reasoned with her. "Men love blow jobs. It's different from being jerked off or fucking someone; it's something in between." He searched for the words. At last, he added, "It gives you a sense of domination and being spoiled in some lustful ways."

Her face found a deeper shade of red. "You really want to lick my pussy?" *He can't want to do this? I mean, his face being down there? I mean…*

CJ stood and leaned over her. His lips tickled at her ear as his hard cock pushed against her thigh. "Baby girl, I don't just want to lick it." His cock jumped, pressing harder against her thigh. "I want to taste and eat it like my favorite dessert." He pulled away to kneel once more. "Eyes on me," he demanded, kissing down her thigh.

She watched, shivers of provocation washing over her with each touch. He glanced up on occasion to make sure her eyes were on him. His lips worked up her inner thigh until the heat of his breath washed over her pussy. *My God, was I always this sensitive down there!* She braced herself as he hooked his arms under and around her legs and pulled her to the edge of the chair. She yelped, placing her hands on top of his shoulders.

"That won't be enough to stop me," he warned with a lustful growl.

The silken heat of his tongue slipped between her folds, and she held her breath. Her body arched, only giving his tongue a chance to lick stronger before the tip of it circled her clit. She squeaked, unsure how to express the new sensation tingling and buzzing through her like electric shock filled with bliss. He moaned into her pussy, and she exhaled. For a moment, she forgot how to breathe as his tongue licked and circled her clit. The pleasurable sensations were unlike anything she had experienced before. He stopped, meeting her wide-eyed glare as she remembered to inhale once more.

"Shall I continue?" He lapped out his tongue and flicked her clit, making her body jolt.

"Y-Yes," she stammered. "Don't stop, I want to—"

A shriek escaped her as his lips wrapped around her clit, sucking long and hard. Her hands fumbled, unsure what to do until, at last, fingers tangled with hair. She jerked him back, and he grinned up at her as she panted, trying to find her words and thoughts. The shot of pleasure overwhelming and addictive. *I want more but...*

"Gentle," she demanded, fingers gripping his hair tight.

"There she is," he cooed, licking his lips. "I was wondering where my mistress was."

A smirk crossed her face, the game with his suckling was back in play with higher stakes. She lowered him back between her thighs. *That's right, I'm in control here.* His tongue licked her opening, and she moaned, trying her best to keep her legs open as she allowed him to return to his fun. She reached above, gripping the top of the chair to fight the urge to pull him away. *I want to see how it feels to cum like this. To get off on his mouth while he—* His tongue pushed inside, and her breath caught once more. *I love the way the way he wiggles inside, tasting me before licking up to my clit.* She could hear how he sucked and smacked like eating a wet dessert.

The tingling buzz built up, and she rocked her hips against his face. He moaned, and her toes curled. Thighs shook as the oncoming orgasm edged closer. Her entire body was on fire with delight and desire like nothing she had ever experienced. Again, his tongue dove inside her, and she gasped. A hand released her thigh, and his tongue returned to circling her clit. She glared down in time to catch his gaze. Fingers slipped in, stroking hard and fast. Before she could gather herself, his lips wrapped around her clit, sucking hard and flicking it violently. She bucked. *Holy hell, I've been missing out!* A squeal of pleasure escaped her as she came. He pulled back, his finger replacing his tongue as she squirted, hard and wet.

14

The People Called Him Wizard

CJ

CJ didn't give her a moment of reprieve. He rammed his hard cock inside her drenched, tight pussy. She cried out in ecstasy as he fucked her, keeping her orgasm exploding as he groaned. Her pussy was hot and on fire in the moment, and she pulled him down to her. Their lips pressed together, opening for one another. His cock jumped as her tongue met his, moaning as she tasted herself. As he pounded her, she broke off the kiss, tilting her head back. He bit his lip. *Hold out a little longer. I don't want to cum just yet. I want to see her in the throes of passion a little longer.*

Pulling out, he started to kiss his way down her body. Suckling on a nipple, his fingers dipped in and out of her. The sounds of her breath hitching goaded him to keep going—to not let a moment of his lustful conquest waiver. *She will know the depths of my love for her.* Another cry escaped her as he made her cum yet again. The onslaught would be something she would never forget. *To be able to be the first to give her this much pleasure.* His heart fluttered as he let go of her nipple with a pop.

Once more, he knelt between her thighs and licked her pussy. She inhaled swiftly as her body lurched forward and arched. He was hungry to give her all the pleasure he could fathom. She grinded against his tongue, and he moaned into her. Legs shuddered in reply. Suckling on her swollen pink pearl, he thrusted fingers in and out of her pulsing channel. Her thighs and his face were slick with his efforts, egging him on as he pounded her.

Looking up, she arched her body, her fingers were white-knuckled where they gripped the chair. "Cum again for me," he commanded. "Cum for me." Another hitch to her breath, and he used his other hand to rub her jewel. "Be a good girl now," he cooed, moaning as his fingers pleased and teased her. "Cum for me, Mary."

"Fuck!" she shouted before bucking once more. "Fuck me! Fuck me right now!"

"I am," he teased.

"I want—" Her breath caught, and she moaned as she orgasmed again, panting. "I want your cock," she breathed.

He retreated, standing as he stroked his cock. "You sure you're ready for this."

"Yes, please." She lay haphazardly across the chair, trying to catch her breath. "I've never wanted a cock inside me so badly in all my life."

"Don't I need to cum for you to show I don't need you?" He smirked, watching her thighs close and rub against one another—a sign she was still riding out her last orgasm. "Prove to you I'm not in distress?"

"Don't you dare," she guffawed, her breasts heaving up and down with her heavy breathing. "I believe you. I just want you to fuck me so badly. I want you inside me," she pleaded.

"Ah, then you're ready for the next thing you asked of me." Wiping his mouth, he motioned for her to flip around. "As I recall, you also promised you would bend over for me."

A smile spread across her face, and she shook her head. "You're a ridiculous lover."

Legs wobbling, she managed to turn herself, knees against the edge of the chair while her palms sunk into the seat cushion. CJ's hands gripped her hips firmly. His heart fluttered seeing how her body curved in and out, the way her spine led his gaze to the mess of hair, and how she peeked over her shoulder at him. He rocked his hips forward, rubbing his cock against the wet heat of her pussy, the flesh swollen and throbbing from his efforts. He bit his lip, thinking before he decided to speak up.

"Look, I don't know if I can pull out in time if we do this." He rocked slow, his cock riding against her opening and growing slicker with each pass. "You're so tight and wet, it's going to take everything I have not to be a two-pump chump," he laughed. "Never in my life," he muttered to himself.

"I want you to cum inside," she confessed.

His heart leapt to his throat. "Um, but if that happens, what if—"

"You love me, right?" She swallowed and rocked her on hips to slide across his cock.

"Y-Yes." He squinted his eyes.

"I..." She searched his face. "It's not the orgasms talking." They smirked at one another. "I love you, CJ. Like I can see settling with you and—"

Reaching down, he guided his cock inside her. "Fucking amazing."

She arched as a shriek escaped her lips. His rock-hard shaft pushed deeper inside her with each swift thrust. Her breasts bounced with each knock on his hilt. They both began to moan, his balls slapping against her with each forward thrust.

"Fuck!" she shrieked. "CJ! Cum for me!"

He groaned, pushing hard into her. Her pussy convulsed, tightened on his shaft, and he lost it. He came hard, letting his own cry of pleasure escape. His cock bumped and jolted with each spurt as she throbbed with her own orgasm. *I've never peaked at the same time as my lover before...* He tried to retreat, but both jolted, and he froze. *Shit. I'm too sensitive to move just yet. Holy hell.*

Swallowing, she stuttered, "That was amazing."

"Yeah, yeah it was," he agreed, "but I can't move."

She shook her head, laughing a little before agreeing. "Me neither."

Panting, he repeated, "I love you, Mary Emrys."

"And I love you, CJ," she breathed.

The sound of someone falling brought their eyes back to the fireplace. The wooden mirror from the closet was beside it, and Timmy waited with a change of clothes for them in his hands.

"What the fuck?" CJ marveled, scooping Mary into his arms to shield her. "How the hell did you get in here?"

"Ah, about that." Timmy laid the clothes on the opposite chair and turned away, though he could still see CJ in the mirror. "You've been missing for a month, so I came to make sure you weren't ... lost?" he offered, smirking. "But I see you had other plans."

"What about Jason?" CJ used a foot to slide his tuxedo jacket over to cover Mary.

"He's been dealt with." Timmy motioned with a hand. "It seems the gala was an unsanctioned fae ritual meant to drain the magic from a wizard or magic holder. Highly illegal. When

Sir Gawain appeared, everyone scattered." Clearing his throat, he then revealed, "And thanks to a ragtag crew of a wraith, poltergeist, and pukwudgie, Jason was arrested by the fairyland officials."

"What's a pukwudgie?" whispered Mary.

"No fucking clue," replied CJ before speaking louder. "Thank you, but if you don't mind, can we get dressed before leaving."

"Oh! Certainly, by all means." Timmy smirked. "We pukwudgie just like a little harmless fun, so I'm glad to see this ended well like I intended. The mirror is safe, and the magic is now yours to control, CJ. Use it wisely, heir to Vivien's magic."

"Thanks…" He watched as Timmy left through the mirror.

"So, the mirror is yours?" Mary gave him an unsteady gaze.

"Like you, I had no clue until all this started to happen." He kissed the top of her head. "I guess we get to discover more about this together, my little cambion who craves the little death."

She hugged him. "Thank you for breaking the curse."

"Someone had to end the blood feud between Merlin and Vivien." He rubbed the back of his neck, brow high. "Who knew we could fuck our way to a solution."

She punched his arm, grabbing the clothes. "You need to fill me in on the details. For now, I want the fuck out of this mirror."

"Good point."

Epilogue

Jason sat in a mirrored cube. He had been caught doing ill to another magical being—something which never sat well with many ruling bodies. *At least I didn't get caught by the Yetis. I would have been torn limb from limb.* Sitting on the prison bed that made up half the cell space, he balled his fists. *Who knew CJ would figure out he could summon and control the mirror. Damn you, Vivien. You conniving harlot!* All he could do was stare down the reflection of himself—a melted version of Jason's face thanks to being disconnected from the human world.

"You can't do this to me!" he shouted, knowing the wardens could indeed hear him. "A changeling must be connected to the human world or it risks dying!" he warned.

"You act like we don't know that," Gawain chuckled, appearing in the reflection. "Listen, we thought long and hard, no pun intended, about this, and we determined a great means of keeping you connected."

"What's taking so long, old man," Jason sneered as an eye drooped further. "I'm melting already. My death will be nearing in a matter of hours. Granted, it beats staying here," he spat.

"Patience. These matters take time." Clearing his throat, he continued his explanation, "We needed permission, and it took some convincing. Someone closer or connected to you works best, no?"

"Convincing? From whom?" Jason gave a disgusted look. "I don't want to be visited by anyone! Unless... Did Chelsea offer?"

"Lord no, we are still hunting for that one," grunted Gawain in annoyance.

"I will not let just anyone see me this way." Jason stood, tapping on the mirror in anger.

"Well, we couldn't have you shifting to be their doppelganger to escape either," agreed Gawain. "But considering your love for mirrors..."

Jason's scowl faltered, and his eyes widened. "You wouldn't?"

"Look, there are fae in prison who would love access to something like this." Gawain smirked. "Consider it a means to ... make serving your *hard* time here a little more ... pleasurable. It will keep you from becoming a complete puddle on the floor."

"You can't do this to me!" Jason beat on the mirror.

The reflection shifted, and he found himself staring down from a ceiling mirror onto a bed. As the couple came into focus, he recognized them immediately: *Mary and CJ.* Dread filled him as they stared up at the mirror with a hint of hesitation across their faces. They looked to one another, whispering. Jason paled. He could hear them loud and clear.

"Are we sure about this?" Mary furrowed her brow.

"Look, the guy will die without it." CJ tried to not laugh. "I think he fucking deserves it. How many times did you watch someone fuck in view of a mirror while stuck there?"

Mary winced, shaking her head. "Don't remind me."

"As I see it, we're showing him mercy," offered CJ.

"NO!" screeched Jason, his voice breaking as his melted parts started to slip back into place. "ANYTHING BUT THIS!"

"Well, I guess it's not like he hasn't seen me naked or in the throes of passion," she reasoned to herself.

"That's the spirit," cooed CJ, tossing the covers to the side to reveal they were already naked.

"CJ!" Mary glanced up at the mirror, face blushing. "He's watching, isn't he?"

"Who fucking cares?" Her face and body flushed red. "Have I told you how good you look in red," he moaned into her neck. "Let me show him how to treat the girl of one's dreams."

Mary laughed, cupping CJ's face. "Is this when you confess you like other people watching you get off?"

"What can I say," he nuzzled into her ear and whispered, "It's quite the turn on when I do it with you in front of the mirror."

"Don't you mean Jason," she added flatly.

"That's just the bonus." He rolled her flat on her back, straddling her. "Now, where shall I begin?" His fingers slid across her lips. "With a kiss? Or perhaps…" He paused as he crawled backward and groped her breasts. "Nipples? No, no I want to hear you scream loud enough to shake the mirrors."

Pushing her thighs apart, he bowed his head between them as pounding on the mirror egged him on.

Original Lyrical Poem

IDYLLS OF THE KING, MERLIN AND VIVIEN

By Alfred Lord Tennyson

A storm was coming, but the winds were still,
And in the wild woods of Broceliande,
Before an oak, so hollow, huge and old
It looked a tower of ivied masonwork,
At Merlin's feet the wily Vivien lay.

For he that always bare in bitter grudge
The slights of Arthur and his Table, Mark
The Cornish King, had heard a wandering voice,
A minstrel of Caerleon by strong storm
Blown into shelter at Tintagil, say
That out of naked knightlike purity
Sir Lancelot worshipt no unmarried girl
But the great Queen herself, fought in her name,
Sware by her--vows like theirs, that high in heaven
Love most, but neither marry, nor are given
In marriage, angels of our Lord's report.

He ceased, and then--for Vivien sweetly said
(She sat beside the banquet nearest Mark),
"And is the fair example followed, Sir,
In Arthur's household?"--answered innocently:

Ay, by some few--ay, truly--youths that hold
It more beseems the perfect virgin knight
To worship woman as true wife beyond

All hopes of gaining, than as maiden girl.
They place their pride in Lancelot and the Queen.
So passionate for an utter purity
Beyond the limit of their bond, are these,
For Arthur bound them not to singleness.
Brave hearts and clean! and yet--God guide them--young."

Then Mark was half in heart to hurl his cup
Straight at the speaker, but forebore: he rose
To leave the hall, and, Vivien following him,
Turned to her: "Here are snakes within the grass;
And you methinks, O Vivien, save ye fear
The monkish manhood, and the mask of pure
Worn by this court, can stir them till they sting."

And Vivien answered, smiling scornfully,
"Why fear? because that fostered at *thy* court
I savour of thy--virtues? fear them? no.
As Love, if Love be perfect, casts out fear,
So Hate, if Hate be perfect, casts out fear.
My father died in battle against the King,
My mother on his corpse in open field;
She bore me there, for born from death was I
Among the dead and sown upon the wind--
And then on thee! and shown the truth betimes,
That old true filth, and bottom of the well,
Where Truth is hidden. Gracious lessons thine
And maxims of the mud! 'This Arthur pure!
Great Nature through the flesh herself hath made
Gives him the lie! There is no being pure,
My cherub; saith not Holy Writ the same?'--
If I were Arthur, I would have thy blood.
Thy blessing, stainless King! I bring thee back,

When I have ferreted out their burrowings,
The hearts of all this Order in mine hand--
Ay--so that fate and craft and folly close,
Perchance, one curl of Arthur's golden beard.
To me this narrow grizzled fork of thine
Is cleaner-fashioned--Well, I loved thee first,
That warps the wit."

Loud laughed the graceless Mark.
But Vivien, into Camelot stealing, lodged
Low in the city, and on a festal day
When Guinevere was crossing the great hall
Cast herself down, knelt to the Queen, and wailed.

Why kneel ye there? What evil have ye wrought?
Rise!" and the damsel bidden rise arose
And stood with folded hands and downward eyes
Of glancing corner, and all meekly said,
"None wrought, but suffered much, an orphan maid!
My father died in battle for thy King,
My mother on his corpse--in open field,
The sad sea-sounding wastes of Lyonnesse--
Poor wretch--no friend!--and now by Mark the King
For that small charm of feature mine, pursued--
If any such be mine--I fly to thee.
Save, save me thou--Woman of women--thine
The wreath of beauty, thine the crown of power,
Be thine the balm of pity, O Heaven's own white
Earth-angel, stainless bride of stainless King--
Help, for he follows! take me to thyself!
O yield me shelter for mine innocency
Among thy maidens!"

Here her slow sweet eyes
Fear-tremulous, but humbly hopeful, rose
Fixt on her hearer's, while the Queen who stood
All glittering like May sunshine on May leaves
In green and gold, and plumed with green replied,
"Peace, child! of overpraise and overblame
We choose the last. Our noble Arthur, him
Ye scarce can overpraise, will hear and know.
Nay--we believe all evil of thy Mark--
Well, we shall test thee farther; but this hour
We ride a-hawking with Sir Lancelot.
He hath given us a fair falcon which he trained;
We go to prove it. Bide ye here the while."

She past; and Vivien murmured after Go!
I bide the while." Then through the portal-arch
Peering askance, and muttering broke-wise,
As one that labours with an evil dream,
Beheld the Queen and Lancelot get to horse.

Is that the Lancelot? goodly--ay, but gaunt:
Courteous--amends for gauntness--takes her hand--
That glance of theirs, but for the street, had been
A clinging kiss--how hand lingers in hand!
Let go at last!--they ride away--to hawk
For waterfowl. Royaller game is mine.
For such a supersensual sensual bond
As that gray cricket chirpt of at our hearth--
Touch flax with flame--a glance will serve--the liars!
Ah little rat that borest in the dyke
Thy hole by night to let the boundless deep
Down upon far-off cities while they dance--
Or dream--of thee they dreamed not--nor of me

These--ay, but each of either: ride, and dream
The mortal dream that never yet was mine--
Ride, ride and dream until ye wake--to me!
Then, narrow court and lubber King, farewell!
For Lancelot will be gracious to the rat,
And our wise Queen, if knowing that I know,
Will hate, loathe, fear--but honour me the more."

Yet while they rode together down the plain,
Their talk was all of training, terms of art,
Diet and seeling, jesses, leash and lure.
"She is too noble" he said "to check at pies,
Nor will she rake: there is no baseness in her."
Here when the Queen demanded as by chance
"Know ye the stranger woman?" "Let her be,"
Said Lancelot and unhooded casting off
The goodly falcon free; she towered; her bells,
Tone under tone, shrilled; and they lifted up
Their eager faces, wondering at the strength,
Boldness and royal knighthood of the bird
Who pounced her quarry and slew it. Many a time
As once--of old--among the flowers--they rode.

But Vivien half-forgotten of the Queen
Among her damsels broidering sat, heard, watched
And whispered: through the peaceful court she crept
And whispered: then as Arthur in the highest
Leavened the world, so Vivien in the lowest,
Arriving at a time of golden rest,
And sowing one ill hint from ear to ear,
While all the heathen lay at Arthur's feet,
And no quest came, but all was joust and play,
Leavened his hall. They heard and let her be.

Thereafter as an enemy that has left
Death in the living waters, and withdrawn,
The wily Vivien stole from Arthur's court.

She hated all the knights, and heard in thought
Their lavish comment when her name was named.
For once, when Arthur walking all alone,
Vext at a rumour issued from herself
Of some corruption crept among his knights,
Had met her, Vivien, being greeted fair,
Would fain have wrought upon his cloudy mood
With reverent eyes mock-loyal, shaken voice,
And fluttered adoration, and at last
With dark sweet hints of some who prized him more
Than who should prize him most; at which the King
Had gazed upon her blankly and gone by:
But one had watched, and had not held his peace:
It made the laughter of an afternoon
That Vivien should attempt the blameless King.
And after that, she set herself to gain
Him, the most famous man of all those times,
Merlin, who knew the range of all their arts,
Had built the King his havens, ships, and halls,
Was also Bard, and knew the starry heavens;
The people called him Wizard; whom at first
She played about with slight and sprightly talk,
And vivid smiles, and faintly-venomed points
Of slander, glancing here and grazing there;
And yielding to his kindlier moods, the Seer
Would watch her at her petulance, and play,
Even when they seemed unloveable, and laugh
As those that watch a kitten; thus he grew
Tolerant of what he half disdained, and she,

Perceiving that she was but half disdained,
Began to break her sports with graver fits,
Turn red or pale, would often when they met
Sigh fully, or all-silent gaze upon him
With such a fixt devotion, that the old man,
Though doubtful, felt the flattery, and at times
Would flatter his own wish in age for love,
And half believe her true: for thus at times
He wavered; but that other clung to him,
Fixt in her will, and so the seasons went.

Then fell on Merlin a great melancholy;
He walked with dreams and darkness, and he found
A doom that ever poised itself to fall,
An ever-moaning battle in the mist,
World-war of dying flesh against the life,
Death in all life and lying in all love,
The meanest having power upon the highest,
And the high purpose broken by the worm.

So leaving Arthur's court he gained the beach;
There found a little boat, and stept into it;
And Vivien followed, but he marked her not.
She took the helm and he the sail; the boat
Drave with a sudden wind across the deeps
And touching Breton sands, they disembarked.
And then she followed Merlin all the way,
Even to the wild woods of Broceliande.
For Merlin once had told her of a charm,
The which if any wrought on anyone
With woven paces and with waving arms,
The man so wrought on ever seemed to lie
Closed in the four walls of a hollow tower,

From which was no escape for evermore;
And none could find that man for evermore,
Nor could he see but him who wrought the charm
Coming and going, and he lay as dead
And lost to life and use and name and fame.
And Vivien ever sought to work the charm
Upon the great Enchanter of the Time,
As fancying that her glory would be great
According to his greatness whom she quenched.

There lay she all her length and kissed his feet,
As if in deepest reverence and in love.
A twist of gold was round her hair; a robe
Of samite without price, that more exprest
Than hid her, clung about her lissome limbs,
In colour like the satin-shining palm
On sallows in the windy gleams of March:
And while she kissed them, crying, "Trample me,
Dear feet, that I have followed through the world,
And I will pay you worship; tread me down
And I will kiss you for it;" he was mute:
So dark a forethought rolled about his brain,
As on a dull day in an Ocean cave
The blind wave feeling round his long sea-hall
In silence: wherefore, when she lifted up
A face of sad appeal, and spake and said,
"O Merlin, do ye love me?" and again,
"O Merlin, do ye love me?" and once more,
"Great Master, do ye love me?" he was mute.
And lissome Vivien, holding by his heel,
Writhed toward him, slided up his knee and sat,
Behind his ankle twined her hollow feet
Together, curved an arm about his neck,

95

Clung like a snake; and letting her left hand
Droop from his mighty shoulder, as a leaf,
Made with her right a comb of pearl to part
The lists of such a beard as youth gone out
Had left in ashes: then he spoke and said,
Not looking at her, "Who are wise in love
Love most, say least," and Vivien answered quick,
"I saw the little elf-god eyeless once
In Arthur's arras hall at Camelot:
But neither eyes nor tongue--O stupid child!
Yet you are wise who say it; let me think
Silence is wisdom: I am silent then,
And ask no kiss;" then adding all at once,
"And lo, I clothe myself with wisdom," drew
The vast and shaggy mantle of his beard
Across her neck and bosom to her knee,
And called herself a gilded summer fly
Caught in a great old tyrant spider's web,
Who meant to eat her up in that wild wood
Without one word. So Vivien called herself,
But rather seemed a lovely baleful star
Veiled in gray vapour; till he sadly smiled:
"To what request for what strange boon," he said,
"Are these your pretty tricks and fooleries,
O Vivien, the preamble? yet my thanks,
For these have broken up my melancholy."

And Vivien answered smiling saucily,
"What, O my Master, have ye found your voice?
I bid the stranger welcome. Thanks at last!
But yesterday you never opened lip,
Except indeed to drink: no cup had we:
In mine own lady palms I culled the spring

That gathered trickling dropwise from the cleft,
And made a pretty cup of both my hands
And offered you it kneeling: then you drank
And knew no more, nor gave me one poor word;
O no more thanks than might a goat have given
With no more sign of reverence than a beard.
And when we halted at that other well,
And I was faint to swooning, and you lay
Foot-gilt with all the blossom-dust of those
Deep meadows we had traversed, did you know
That Vivien bathed your feet before her own?
And yet no thanks: and all through this wild wood
And all this morning when I fondled you:
Boon, ay, there was a boon, one not so strange--
How had I wronged you? surely ye are wise,
But such a silence is more wise than kind."

And Merlin locked his hand in hers and said:
"O did ye never lie upon the shore,
And watch the curled white of the coming wave
Glassed in the slippery sand before it breaks?
Even such a wave, but not so pleasurable,
Dark in the glass of some presageful mood,
Had I for three days seen, ready to fall.
And then I rose and fled from Arthur's court
To break the mood. You followed me unasked;
And when I looked, and saw you following still,
My mind involved yourself the nearest thing
In that mind-mist: for shall I tell you truth?
You seemed that wave about to break upon me
And sweep me from my hold upon the world,
My use and name and fame. Your pardon, child.
Your pretty sports have brightened all again.

And ask your boon, for boon I owe you thrice,
Once for wrong done you by confusion, next
For thanks it seems till now neglected, last
For these your dainty gambols: wherefore ask;
And take this boon so strange and not so strange."

And Vivien answered smiling mournfully:
"O not so strange as my long asking it,
Not yet so strange as you yourself are strange,
Nor half so strange as that dark mood of yours.
I ever feared ye were not wholly mine;
And see, yourself have owned ye did me wrong.
The people call you prophet: let it be:
But not of those that can expound themselves.
Take Vivien for expounder; she will call
That three-days-long presageful gloom of yours
No presage, but the same mistrustful mood
That makes you seem less noble than yourself,
Whenever I have asked this very boon,
Now asked again: for see you not, dear love,
That such a mood as that, which lately gloomed
Your fancy when ye saw me following you,
Must make me fear still more you are not mine,
Must make me yearn still more to prove you mine,
And make me wish still more to learn this charm
Of woven paces and of waving hands,
As proof of trust. O Merlin, teach it me.
The charm so taught will charm us both to rest.
For, grant me some slight power upon your fate,
I, feeling that you felt me worthy trust,
Should rest and let you rest, knowing you mine.
And therefore be as great as ye are named.
Not muffled round with selfish reticence.

How hard you look and how denyingly!
O, if you think this wickedness in me,
That I should prove it on you unawares,
That makes me passing wrathful; then our bond
Had best be loosed for ever: but think or not,
By Heaven that hears I tell you the clean truth,
As clean as blood of babes, as white as milk:
O Merlin, may this earth, if ever I,
If these unwitty wandering wits of mine,
Even in the jumbled rubbish of a dream,
Have tript on such conjectural treachery--
May this hard earth cleave to the Nadir hell
Down, down, and close again, and nip me flat,
If I be such a traitress. Yield my boon,
Till which I scarce can yield you all I am;
And grant my re-reiterated wish,
The great proof of your love: because I think,
However wise, ye hardly know me yet."

And Merlin loosed his hand from hers and said,
"I never was less wise, however wise,
Too curious Vivien, though you talk of trust,
Than when I told you first of such a charm.
Yea, if ye talk of trust I tell you this,
Too much I trusted when I told you that,
And stirred this vice in you which ruined man
Through woman the first hour; for howsoe'er
In children a great curiousness be well,
Who have to learn themselves and all the world,
In you, that are no child, for still I find
Your face is practised when I spell the lines,
I call it,--well, I will not call it vice:
But since you name yourself the summer fly,

I well could wish a cobweb for the gnat,
That settles, beaten back, and beaten back
Settles, till one could yield for weariness:
But since I will not yield to give you power
Upon my life and use and name and fame,
Why will ye never ask some other boon?
Yea, by God's rood, I trusted you too much."

And Vivien, like the tenderest-hearted maid
That ever bided tryst at village stile,
Made answer, either eyelid wet with tears:
"Nay, Master, be not wrathful with your maid;
Caress her: let her feel herself forgiven
Who feels no heart to ask another boon.
I think ye hardly know the tender rhyme
Of 'trust me not at all or all in all.'
I heard the great Sir Lancelot sing it once,
And it shall answer for me. Listen to it.

In Love, if Love be Love, if Love be ours,
Faith and unfaith can ne'er be equal powers:
Unfaith in aught is want of faith in all.

It is the little rift within the lute,
That by and by will make the music mute,
And ever widening slowly silence all.

The little rift within the lover's lute
Or little pitted speck in garnered fruit,
That rotting inward slowly moulders all.

It is not worth the keeping: let it go:
But shall it? answer, darling, answer, no.
And trust me not at all or all in all.'

O Master, do ye love my tender rhyme?"

And Merlin looked and half believed her true,
So tender was her voice, so fair her face,
So sweetly gleamed her eyes behind her tears
Like sunlight on the plain behind a shower:
And yet he answered half indignantly:

Far other was the song that once I heard
By this huge oak, sung nearly where we sit:
For here we met, some ten or twelve of us,
To chase a creature that was current then
In these wild woods, the hart with golden horns.
It was the time when first the question rose
About the founding of a Table Round,
That was to be, for love of God and men
And noble deeds, the flower of all the world.
And each incited each to noble deeds.
And while we waited, one, the youngest of us,
We could not keep him silent, out he flashed,
And into such a song, such fire for fame,
Such trumpet-blowings in it, coming down
To such a stern and iron-clashing close,
That when he stopt we longed to hurl together,
And should have done it; but the beauteous beast
Scared by the noise upstarted at our feet,
And like a silver shadow slipt away
Through the dim land; and all day long we rode
Through the dim land against a rushing wind,

That glorious roundel echoing in our ears,
And chased the flashes of his golden horns
Until they vanished by the fairy well
That laughs at iron--as our warriors did--
Where children cast their pins and nails, and cry,
'Laugh, little well!' but touch it with a sword,
It buzzes fiercely round the point; and there
We lost him: such a noble song was that.
But, Vivien, when you sang me that sweet rhyme,
I felt as though you knew this cursèd charm,
Were proving it on me, and that I lay
And felt them slowly ebbing, name and fame."

And Vivien answered smiling mournfully:
"O mine have ebbed away for evermore,
And all through following you to this wild wood,
Because I saw you sad, to comfort you.
Lo now, what hearts have men! they never mount
As high as woman in her selfless mood.
And touching fame, howe'er ye scorn my song,
Take one verse more--the lady speaks it--this:

My name, once mine, now thine, is closelier mine,
For fame, could fame be mine, that fame were thine,
And shame, could shame be thine, that shame were mine.
So trust me not at all or all in all.'

Says she not well? and there is more--this rhyme
Is like the fair pearl-necklace of the Queen,
That burst in dancing, and the pearls were spilt;
Some lost, some stolen, some as relics kept.
But nevermore the same two sister pearls
Ran down the silken thread to kiss each other

On her white neck--so is it with this rhyme:
It lives dispersedly in many hands,
And every minstrel sings it differently;
'Man dreams of Fame while woman wakes to love.'
Yea! Love, though Love were of the grossest, carves
A portion from the solid present, eats
And uses, careless of the rest; but Fame,
The Fame that follows death is nothing to us;
And what is Fame in life but half-disfame,
And counterchanged with darkness? ye yourself
Know well that Envy calls you Devil's son,
And since ye seem the Master of all Art,
They fain would make you Master of all vice."

And Merlin locked his hand in hers and said,
"I once was looking for a magic weed,
And found a fair young squire who sat alone,
Had carved himself a knightly shield of wood,
And then was painting on it fancied arms,
Azure, an Eagle rising or, the Sun
In dexter chief; the scroll 'I follow fame.'
And speaking not, but leaning over him,
I took his brush and blotted out the bird,
And made a Gardner putting in a graff,
With this for motto, 'Rather use than fame.'
You should have seen him blush; but afterwards
He made a stalwart knight. O Vivien,
For you, methinks you think you love me well;
For me, I love you somewhat; rest: and Love
Should have some rest and pleasure in himself,
Not ever be too curious for a boon,
Too prurient for a proof against the grain
Of him ye say ye love: but Fame with men,

Being but ampler means to serve mankind,
Should have small rest or pleasure in herself,
But work as vassal to the larger love,
That dwarfs the petty love of one to one.
Use gave me Fame at first, and Fame again
Increasing gave me use. Lo, there my boon!
What other? for men sought to prove me vile,
Because I fain had given them greater wits:
And then did Envy call me Devil's son:
The sick weak beast seeking to help herself
By striking at her better, missed, and brought
Her own claw back, and wounded her own heart.
Sweet were the days when I was all unknown,
But when my name was lifted up, the storm
Brake on the mountain and I cared not for it.
Right well know I that Fame is half-disfame,
Yet needs must work my work. That other fame,
To one at least, who hath not children, vague,
The cackle of the unborn about the grave,
I cared not for it: a single misty star,
Which is the second in a line of stars
That seem a sword beneath a belt of three,
I never gazed upon it but I dreamt
Of some vast charm concluded in that star
To make fame nothing. Wherefore, if I fear,
Giving you power upon me through this charm,
That you might play me falsely, having power,
However well ye think ye love me now
(As sons of kings loving in pupilage
Have turned to tyrants when they came to power)
I rather dread the loss of use than fame;
If you--and not so much from wickedness,
As some wild turn of anger, or a mood

Of overstrained affection, it may be,
To keep me all to your own self,--or else
A sudden spurt of woman's jealousy,--
Should try this charm on whom ye say ye love."

And Vivien answered smiling as in wrath:
"Have I not sworn? I am not trusted. Good!
Well, hide it, hide it; I shall find it out;
And being found take heed of Vivien.
A woman and not trusted, doubtless I
Might feel some sudden turn of anger born
Of your misfaith; and your fine epithet
Is accurate too, for this full love of mine
Without the full heart back may merit well
Your term of overstrained. So used as I,
My daily wonder is, I love at all.
And as to woman's jealousy, O why not?
O to what end, except a jealous one,
And one to make me jealous if I love,
Was this fair charm invented by yourself?
I well believe that all about this world
Ye cage a buxom captive here and there,
Closed in the four walls of a hollow tower
From which is no escape for evermore."

Then the great Master merrily answered her:
"Full many a love in loving youth was mine;
I needed then no charm to keep them mine
But youth and love; and that full heart of yours
Whereof ye prattle, may now assure you mine;
So live uncharmed. For those who wrought it first,
The wrist is parted from the hand that waved,
The feet unmortised from their ankle-bones

Who paced it, ages back: but will ye hear
The legend as in guerdon for your rhyme?

There lived a king in the most Eastern East,
Less old than I, yet older, for my blood
Hath earnest in it of far springs to be.
A tawny pirate anchored in his port,
Whose bark had plundered twenty nameless isles;
And passing one, at the high peep of dawn,
He saw two cities in a thousand boats
All fighting for a woman on the sea.
And pushing his black craft among them all,
He lightly scattered theirs and brought her off,
With loss of half his people arrow-slain;
A maid so smooth, so white, so wonderful,
They said a light came from her when she moved:
And since the pirate would not yield her up,
The King impaled him for his piracy;
Then made her Queen: but those isle-nurtured eyes
Waged such unwilling though successful war
On all the youth, they sickened; councils thinned,
And armies waned, for magnet-like she drew
The rustiest iron of old fighters' hearts;
And beasts themselves would worship; camels knelt
Unbidden, and the brutes of mountain back
That carry kings in castles, bowed black knees
Of homage, ringing with their serpent hands,
To make her smile, her golden ankle-bells.
What wonder, being jealous, that he sent
His horns of proclamation out through all
The hundred under-kingdoms that he swayed
To find a wizard who might teach the King
Some charm, which being wrought upon the Queen

Might keep her all his own: to such a one
He promised more than ever king has given,
A league of mountain full of golden mines,
A province with a hundred miles of coast,
A palace and a princess, all for him:
But on all those who tried and failed, the King
Pronounced a dismal sentence, meaning by it
To keep the list low and pretenders back,
Or like a king, not to be trifled with--
Their heads should moulder on the city gates.
And many tried and failed, because the charm
Of nature in her overbore their own:
And many a wizard brow bleached on the walls:
And many weeks a troop of carrion crows
Hung like a cloud above the gateway towers."

And Vivien breaking in upon him, said:
"I sit and gather honey; yet, methinks,
Thy tongue has tript a little: ask thyself.
The lady never made *unwilling* war
With those fine eyes: she had her pleasure in it,
And made her good man jealous with good cause.
And lived there neither dame nor damsel then
Wroth at a lover's loss? were all as tame,
I mean, as noble, as the Queen was fair?
Not one to flirt a venom at her eyes,
Or pinch a murderous dust into her drink,
Or make her paler with a poisoned rose?
Well, those were not our days: but did they find
A wizard? Tell me, was he like to thee?

She ceased, and made her lithe arm round his neck
Tighten, and then drew back, and let her eyes

Speak for her, glowing on him, like a bride's
On her new lord, her own, the first of men.

He answered laughing, Nay, not like to me.
At last they found--his foragers for charms--
A little glassy-headed hairless man,
Who lived alone in a great wild on grass;
Read but one book, and ever reading grew
So grated down and filed away with thought,
So lean his eyes were monstrous; while the skin
Clung but to crate and basket, ribs and spine.
And since he kept his mind on one sole aim,
Nor ever touched fierce wine, nor tasted flesh,
Nor owned a sensual wish, to him the wall
That sunders ghosts and shadow-casting men
Became a crystal, and he saw them through it,
And heard their voices talk behind the wall,
And learnt their elemental secrets, powers
And forces; often o'er the sun's bright eye
Drew the vast eyelid of an inky cloud,
And lashed it at the base with slanting storm;
Or in the noon of mist and driving rain,
When the lake whitened and the pinewood roared,
And the cairned mountain was a shadow, sunned
The world to peace again: here was the man.
And so by force they dragged him to the King.
And then he taught the King to charm the Queen
In such-wise, that no man could see her more,
Nor saw she save the King, who wrought the charm,
Coming and going, and she lay as dead,
And lost all use of life: but when the King
Made proffer of the league of golden mines,
The province with a hundred miles of coast,

The palace and the princess, that old man
Went back to his old wild, and lived on grass,
And vanished, and his book came down to me."

And Vivien answered smiling saucily:
"Ye have the book: the charm is written in it:
Good: take my counsel: let me know it at once:
For keep it like a puzzle chest in chest,
With each chest locked and padlocked thirty-fold,
And whelm all this beneath as vast a mound
As after furious battle turfs the slain
On some wild down above the windy deep,
I yet should strike upon a sudden means
To dig, pick, open, find and read the charm:
Then, if I tried it, who should blame me then?"

And smiling as a master smiles at one
That is not of his school, nor any school
But that where blind and naked Ignorance
Delivers brawling judgments, unashamed,
On all things all day long, he anwered her:

Thou read the book, my pretty Vivien!
O ay, it is but twenty pages long,
But every page having an ample marge,
And every marge enclosing in the midst
A square of text that looks a little blot,
The text no larger than the limbs of fleas;
And every square of text an awful charm,
Writ in a language that has long gone by.
So long, that mountains have arisen since
With cities on their flanks--thou read the book!
And every margin scribbled, crost, and crammed

With comment, densest condensation, hard
To mind and eye; but the long sleepless nights
Of my long life have made it easy to me.
And none can read the text, not even I;
And none can read the comment but myself;
And in the comment did I find the charm.
O, the results are simple; a mere child
Might use it to the harm of anyone,
And never could undo it: ask no more:
For though you should not prove it upon me,
But keep the oath ye sware, ye might, perchance,
Assay it on some one of the Table Round,
And all because ye dream they babble of you."

And Vivien, frowning in true anger, said:
"What dare the full-fed liars say of me?
They ride abroad redressing human wrongs!
They sit with knife in meat and wine in horn!
They bound to holy vows of chastity!
Were I not woman, I could tell a tale.
But you are man, you well can understand
The shame that cannot be explained for shame.
Not one of all the drove should touch me: swine!"

Then answered Merlin careless of her words:
"You breathe but accusation vast and vague,
Spleen-born, I think, and proofless. If ye know,
Set up the charge ye know, to stand or fall!"

And Vivien answered frowning wrathfully:
"O ay, what say ye to Sir Valence, him
Whose kinsman left him watcher o'er his wife
And two fair babes, and went to distant lands;

Was one year gone, and on returning found
Not two but three? there lay the reckling, one
But one hour old! What said the happy sire?
A seven-months' babe had been a truer gift.
Those twelve sweet moons confused his fatherhood."

Then answered Merlin, Nay, I know the tale.
Sir Valence wedded with an outland dame:
Some cause had kept him sundered from his wife:
One child they had: it lived with her: she died:
His kinsman travelling on his own affair
Was charged by Valence to bring home the child.
He brought, not found it therefore: take the truth."

O ay,» said Vivien, overtrue a tale.
What say ye then to sweet Sir Sagramore,
That ardent man? 'to pluck the flower in season,'
So says the song, 'I trow it is no treason.'
O Master, shall we call him overquick
To crop his own sweet rose before the hour?"

And Merlin answered, Overquick art thou
To catch a loathly plume fallen from the wing
Of that foul bird of rapine whose whole prey
Is man's good name: he never wronged his bride.
I know the tale. An angry gust of wind
Puffed out his torch among the myriad-roomed
And many-corridored complexities
Of Arthur's palace: then he found a door,
And darkling felt the sculptured ornament
That wreathen round it made it seem his own;
And wearied out made for the couch and slept,
A stainless man beside a stainless maid;

And either slept, nor knew of other there;
Till the high dawn piercing the royal rose
In Arthur's casement glimmered chastely down,
Blushing upon them blushing, and at once
He rose without a word and parted from her:
But when the thing was blazed about the court,
The brute world howling forced them into bonds,
And as it chanced they are happy, being pure."

O ay,» said Vivien, that were likely too.
What say ye then to fair Sir Percivale
And of the horrid foulness that he wrought,
The saintly youth, the spotless lamb of Christ,
Or some black wether of St. Satan's fold.
What, in the precints of the chapel-yard,
Among the knightly brasses of the graves,
And by the cold Hic Jacets of the dead!"

And Merlin answered careless of her charge,
"A sober man is Percivale and pure;
But once in life was flustered with new wine,
Then paced for coolness in the chapel-yard;
Where one of Satan's shepherdesses caught
And meant to stamp him with her master's mark:
And that he sinned is not believable;
For, look upon his face!--but if he sinned,
The sin that practice burns into the blood,
And not the one dark hour which brings remorse,
Will brand us, after, of whose fold we be:
Or else were he, the holy king, whose hymns
Are chanted in the minster, worse than all.
But is your spleen frothed out, or have ye more?"

And Vivien answered frowning yet in wrath:
"O ay; what say ye to Sir Lancelot, friend
Traitor or true? that commerce with the Queen,
I ask you, is it clamoured by the child,
Or whispered in the corner? do ye know it?"

To which he answered sadly, Yea, I know it.
Sir Lancelot went ambassador, at first,
To fetch her, and she watched him from her walls.
A rumour runs, she took him for the King,
So fixt her fancy on him: let them be.
But have ye no one word of loyal praise
For Arthur, blameless King and stainless man?"

She answered with a low and chuckling laugh:
"Man! is he man at all, who knows and winks?
Sees what his fair bride is and does, and winks?
By which the good King means to blind himself,
And blinds himself and all the Table Round
To all the foulness that they work. Myself
Could call him (were it not for womanhood)
The pretty, popular name such manhood earns,
Could call him the main cause of all their crime;
Yea, were he not crowned King, coward, and fool."

Then Merlin to his own heart, loathing, said:
"O true and tender! O my liege and King!
O selfless man and stainless gentleman,
Who wouldst against thine own eye-witness fain
Have all men true and leal, all women pure;
How, in the mouths of base interpreters,
From over-fineness not intelligible
To things with every sense as false and foul

As the poached filth that floods the middle street,
Is thy white blamelessness accounted blame!"

But Vivien, deeming Merlin overborne
By instance, recommenced , and let her tongue
Rage like a fire among the noblest names,
Polluting, and imputing her whole self,
Defaming and defacing, till she left
Not even Lancelot brave, nor Galahad clean.

Her words had issue other than she willed.
He dragged his eyebrow bushes down, and made
A snowy penthouse for his hollow eyes,
And muttered in himself, "Tell *her* the charm!
So, if she had it, would she rail on me
To snare the next, and if she have it not
So will she rail. What did the wanton say?
'Not mount as high;' we scarce can sink as low:
For men at most differ as Heaven and earth,
But women, worst and best, as Heaven and Hell.
I know the Table Round, my friends of old;
All brave, and many generous, and some chaste.
She cloaks the scar of some repulse with lies;
I well believe she tempted them and failed,
Being so bitter: for fine plots may fail,
Though harlots paint their talk as well as face
With colours of the heart that are not theirs.
I will not let her know: nine tithes of times
Face-flatterer and backbiter are the same.
And they, sweet soul, that most impute a crime
Are pronest to it, and impute themselves,
Wanting the mental range; or low desire
Not to feel lowest makes them level all;

Yea, they would pare the mountain to the plain,
To leave an equal baseness; and in this
Are harlots like the crowd, that if they find
Some stain or blemish in a name of note,
Not grieving that their greatest are so small,
Inflate themselves with some insane delight,
And judge all nature from her feet of clay,
Without the will to lift their eyes, and see
Her godlike head crowned with spiritual fire,
And touching other worlds. I am weary of her."

He spoke in words part heard, in whispers part,
Half-suffocated in the hoary fell
And many-wintered fleece of throat and chin.
But Vivien, gathering somewhat of his mood,
And hearing "harlot" muttered twice or thrice,
Leapt from her session on his lap, and stood
Stiff as a viper frozen; loathsome sight,
How from the rosy lips of life and love,
Flashed the bare grinning skeleton of death!
White was her cheek; sharp breaths of anger puffed
Her fairy nostril out; her hand half-clenched
Went faltering sideways downward to her belt,
And feeling; had she found a dagger there
(For in a wink the false love turns to hate)
She would have stabbed him; but she found it not:
His eye was calm, and suddenly she took
To bitter weeping like a beaten child,
A long, long weeping, not consolable.
Then her false voice made way, broken with sobs:

O crueller than was ever told in tale,
Or sung in song! O vainly lavished love!

O cruel, there was nothing wild or strange,
Or seeming shameful--for what shame in love,
So love be true, and not as yours is--nothing
Poor Vivien had not done to win his trust
Who called her what he called her--all her crime,
All--all--the wish to prove him wholly hers."

She mused a little, and then clapt her hands
Together with a wailing shriek, and said:
"Stabbed through the heart's affections to the heart!
Seethed like the kid in its own mother's milk!
Killed with a word worse than a life of blows!
I thought that he was gentle, being great:
O God, that I had loved a smaller man!
I should have found in him a greater heart.
O, I, that flattering my true passion, saw
The knights, the court, the King, dark in your light,
Who loved to make men darker than they are,
Because of that high pleasure which I had
To seat you sole upon my pedestal
Of worship--I am answered, and henceforth
The course of life that seemed so flowery to me
With you for guide and master, only you,
Becomes the sea-cliff pathway broken short,
And ending in a ruin--nothing left,
But into some low cave to crawl, and there,
If the wolf spare me, weep my life away,
Killed with inutterable unkindliness."

She paused, she turned away, she hung her head,
The snake of gold slid from her hair, the braid
Slipt and uncoiled itself, she wept afresh,
And the dark wood grew darker toward the storm

In silence, while his anger slowly died
Within him, till he let his wisdom go
For ease of heart, and half believed her true:
Called her to shelter, in the hollow oak,
"Come from the storm," and having no reply,
Gazed at the heaving shoulder, and the face
Hand-hidden, as for utmost grief or shame;
Then thrice essayed, by tenderest-touching terms,
To sleek her ruffled peace of mind, in vain.
At last she let herself be conquered by him,
And as the cageling newly flown returns,
The seeming-injured simple-hearted thing
Came to her old perch back, and settled there.
There while she sat, half-falling from his knees,
Half-nestled at his heart, and since he saw
The slow tear creep from her closed eyelid yet,
About her, more in kindness than in love,
The gentle wizard cast a shielding arm.
But she dislinked herself at once and rose,
Her arms upon her breast across, and stood,
A virtuous gentlewoman deeply wronged,
Upright and flushed before him: then she said:

There must be now no passages of love
Betwixt us twain henceforward evermore;
Since, if I be what I am grossly called,
What should be granted which your own gross heart
Would reckon worth the taking? I will go.
In truth, but one thing now--better have died
Thrice than have asked it once--could make me stay--
That proof of trust--so often asked in vain!
How justly, after that vile term of yours,
I find with grief! I might believe you then,

Who knows? once more. Lo! what was once to me
Mere matter of the fancy, now hath grown
The vast necessity of heart and life.
Farewell; think gently of me, for I fear
My fate or folly, passing gayer youth
For one so old, must be to love thee still.
But ere I leave thee let me swear once more
That if I schemed against thy peace in this,
May yon just heaven, that darkens o'er me, send
One flash, that, missing all things else, may make
My scheming brain a cinder, if I lie."

Scarce had she ceased, when out of heaven a bolt
(For now the storm was close above them) struck,
Furrowing a giant oak, and javelining
With darted spikes and splinters of the wood
The dark earth round. He raised his eyes and saw
The tree that shone white-listed through the gloom.
But Vivien, fearing heaven had heard her oath,
And dazzled by the livid-flickering fork,
And deafened with the stammering cracks and claps
That followed, flying back and crying out,
"O Merlin, though you do not love me, save,
Yet save me!" clung to him and hugged him close;
And called him dear protector in her fright,
Nor yet forgot her practice in her fright,
But wrought upon his mood and hugged him close.
The pale blood of the wizard at her touch
Took gayer colours, like an opal warmed.
She blamed herself for telling hearsay tales:
She shook from fear, and for her fault she wept
Of petulancy; she called him lord and liege,
Her seer, her bard, her silver star of eve,

Her God, her Merlin, the one passionate love
Of her whole life; and ever overhead
Bellowed the tempest, and the rotten branch
Snapt in the rushing of the river-rain
Above them; and in change of glare and gloom
Her eyes and neck glittering went and came;
Till now the storm, its burst of passion spent,
Moaning and calling out of other lands,
Had left the ravaged woodland yet once more
To peace; and what should not have been had been,
For Merlin, overtalked and overworn,
Had yielded, told her all the charm, and slept.

Then, in one moment, she put forth the charm
Of woven paces and of waving hands,
And in the hollow oak he lay as dead,
And lost to life and use and name and fame.

Then crying I have made his glory mine,»
And shrieking out "O fool!" the harlot leapt
Adown the forest, and the thicket closed
Behind her, and the forest echoed "fool."

Author Bio

A passionate, award-winning author of fantasy, Honey has turned her aim toward erotica. Blending everyday scenarios and crafting them into steamy, blood-boiling moments for every shade of audience. Whether you want something short and hot like a student-teacher hookup or more paranormal flair like *Sleeping with Sasquatch* with an unexpected bonus, look forward to erotic short stories, novellas, and hopefully a trilogy in the future. Honey's debut erotic short landed No. 3 in urban erotica and continues to satisfy readers time and time again. Be sure to leave her a review and let her know what you think!

More books from
4 Horsemen Publications

Erotica

Ali Whippe
Office Hours
Tutoring Center
Athletics
Extra Credit
Financial Aid
Bound for Release
Fetish Circuit
Now You See Me
Sexual Playground
Swingers
Discovered
XTC College Series Collection

Aria Skylar
Twisted Eros
Seducing Dionysus

Chastity Veldt
Molly in Milwaukee
Irene in Indianapolis
Lydia in Louisville
Natasha in Nashville
Alyssa in Atlanta
Betty in Birmingham
Carrie on Campus
Jackie in Jacksonville
A Humorous Erotica Collection

Dalia Lance
My Home on Whore Island
Slumming It on Slut Street

Training of the Tramp
The Imperfect Perfection
Spring Break
72% Match
It Was Meant To Be... Or Whatever

Honey Cummings
Sleeping with Sasquatch
Cuddling with Chupacabra
Naked with New Jersey Devil
Laying with the Lady in Blue
Wanton Woman in White
Beating it with Bloody Mary
The Erotic Cryptid Collection
Beau and Professor Bestialora
The Goat's Gruff
Goldie and Her Three Beards
Pied Piper's Pipe
Princess Pea's Bed
Pinocchio and the Blow Up Doll
Jack's Beanstalk
Pulling Rapunzel's Hair
The Urban Erotica Fairy Tale
Collection
Curses & Crushes
Queen's Incubus

Nick Savage
The Fairlane Incidents
The Fortunate Finn Fairlane
The Fragile Finn Fairlane
The Complete Package

Discover more at
4HorsemenPublications.com